Julia Magruder

Across the Chasm

Julia Magruder

Across the Chasm

ISBN/EAN: 9783337256012

Printed in Europe, USA, Canada, Australia, Japan

Cover: Foto ©Andreas Hilbeck / pixelio.de

More available books at **www.hansebooks.com**

ACROSS THE CHASM

ACROSS THE CHASM

NEW YORK
CHARLES SCRIBNER'S SONS
1885

Press of J. J. Little & Co.,
New York.

ACROSS THE CHASM.

CHAPTER I.

MARGARET TREVENNON was young and beautiful. Her faithful biographer can say no less, though aware of the possibility that, on this account, the satiated reader of romances may make her acquaintance with a certain degree of reluctance, reflecting upon the two well-worn types—the maiden in the first flush of youth, who is so immaculately lovely as to be extremely improbable, and the maturer female, who is so strong-minded as to be wholly ineligible to romantic situations. If there be only these two classes Miss Trevennon must needs be ranged with the former. Certainly the particular character of her beauty fore-ordained her to romantic situations, although it must be said, on the other hand, that the term "strong-minded" was one which had been more than once applied to her by those who should have known her best.

She lived with her parents on the outskirts of a small Southern town, in a dilapidated old house, that had once been a grand mansion. The days of its splendid hospitality had passed away long since, and as far back as Margaret's memory went the same monotonous tranquillity had pervaded its lofty corridors and spacious rooms. In spite of this, however, it was a pleasant, cheerful home, and the girl's life, up to her nineteenth year, had been passed very happily in it. She had had occasional changes of scene, such as a visit to New Orleans or a brief season at some small Southern watering-place; but she had never been North, and so by birth and circumstance, as well as by instinct and training, she was a genuine Southern girl. The fact that Mr. Trevennon had managed to save from the wreck of his large fortune a small independence, had afforded his daughter the opportunity of seeing something of men and manners beyond her own hearth-stone, and this, together with her varied and miscellaneous reading, gave her a range of vision wider and higher than that enjoyed by the other young people of Bassett, and had imbued her with certain theories and opinions which made them regard her as eccentric.

One bright autumnal day, when the weather was still warm and sunny in this fair Southern climate, Miss Trevennon, clad in an airy white costume, and protected from the sun by a veil and parasol, took her way with the rather quick motions usual with her, down the main street of Bassett. When she reached the corner on which Martin's drug store was situated, she crossed over and passed down on the opposite side ; but, doubly screened as she was, she turned her eyes in that direction and took a hurried survey of the loungers assembled on the pavement. Perhaps it was because her gaze especially sought him out that she saw Charley Somers first. This was a young man who had been her unrequited adorer, hoping against hope, ever since they had gone to the village school together, and Margaret had all her life been trying, in a flashing, impetuous way that she had, to fire him with some of the energy and enthusiasm which she herself possessed so abundantly, and in which this pleasant, easy, indolent young Southerner was so absolutely lacking. Young Somers had come of a long line of affluent and luxurious ancestors, and though cut off from an inheritance in their worldly possessions, he had fallen heir to many of their personal characteristics, which hung about him like fetters of steel.

Although Miss Trevennon hurriedly averted her gaze after that one swift glance, she had received a distinct impression of Mr. Somers' whole manner and attitude, as he sat with his chair tipped back against the wall, his heels caught on its topmost round, his straw hat pushed back from his delicate, indolent face, and a pipe between his lips. In this way he would sit for hours, ringing the changes on the somewhat restricted theme of county politics with the loungers who frequented "Martin's." The mere thought of it, much more the sight, infuriated Miss Trevennon. She could not grow accustomed to it, in spite of long habituation.

As she tripped along, erect and quick, she heard a familiar footstep behind her, and in a moment more was joined by the young man.

"Where are you going?" he said, giving his hat a little careless push and re-settlement, without lifting it from his head. "May I go with you and carry your basket?"

"If you like," said Margaret, distantly, yielding up to him the little white-covered basket. "I am going to see Uncle Mose."

"As usual! What has Uncle Mose done to be so petted? I wish you would treat me with half as much consideration."

"I don't think you entitled to it," she answered. "Uncle Mose is at the end of a long life of continuous, patient labor, and has won a right to my consideration, which you never have. You have often heard me say, of course, that ever since I've been able to form an opinion at all, I've been a thorough-going Abolitionist; but all the same, I think there is virtue in a system which *makes* a man work, whether he wills it or not. Servitude itself seems to me a nobler life than absolute idleness."

"Oh, the same old thing!" said the young man, wearily. "I wonder when you will give up expecting me to be a paragon!"

"I've given it up long ago. I've seen the futility of any such expectation; but I will never give up wishing that you would be a man, and do something worthy of a man."

"You can't say I don't work. I attend to my cases, and am always on hand during court week."

"Provided it doesn't clash with fishing week or hunting week, or any pursuit that happens to offer a more attractive prospect than that of discussing county politics and smoking bad tobacco with some other loungers at ' Martin's ' ! "

"I know I am not what you like," said Somers despondently; "but there is one thing that would make me different. If you would give me some hope for the future——"

"I begged you never to say that again," interrupted Margaret, quickly. "You know how indignant it makes me, and the worst of it is that you really believe it to be true. If you won't do right for right's sake, you would never do it for mine."

He made no answer to her words. But one form of response suggested itself, and to that he knew she was in no mood to listen; so, for the space of a few moments, they walked along in silence. But Margaret's thoughts were very active, and presently she broke out:

"Why, Charley, when I heard you complaining the other day, that the tailor who has a shop opposite you kept you from sleeping in the morning by his violin practice begun at daylight, I remembered how you had told me once that you frequently saw him at his work until after midnight; and do you know what I thought? I thought: I wish to goodness Charley would try to be a little more like him."

"What do you mean?" the young man cried, angrily. "You don't know what you are talking about. Do you think I could ever so far forget myself as to imitate a beastly little Yankee tailor, or to desire to be like him in any way whatever? I can stand a good deal from you, Margaret, but this is a little too much!"

"Of course! His happening to be a Yankee puts him down at once. But I can tell you what it is, Charley, there is one lesson you might profitably learn from him, and that the most important in the world for you. It is, to make something of the powers you have. That poor little man has no possibilities, I suppose, beyond the attainment of a certain degree of skill in making clothing, on the one hand, and learning to play popular airs indifferently on a cracked little fiddle, on the other. But with you, how different it is! Papa says you would be an able lawyer, but for the trifling obstacle that you don't know any law. We all know how well you talk, on those rare occasions on which you become really interested. And as to the other point, the music—oh, Charley, what mightn't your voice become, if you would avail yourself of the means of cultivation within your reach? But no! Your teacher told you that you must practise patiently and continuously to procure its proper development, and this you would not do; it was too troublesome!"

"Trouble apart," said Somers, "the notion does not please me, and I must say I wonder that you, who make such a point of manliness in a man, should favor any one's regularly preparing himself to be the sort of drawing-room pet that one of your trained song-singers is certain to become."

"You *can* say the most aggravating things!" said Margaret. "Is it possible that you can consider it unmanly to cultivate such a gift as that? But what's the use of all this? You don't care."

"No, I don't care much," he answered

slowly. "When a man has one supreme, paramount care forever possessing him, and is constantly being told that the object of his desires is beyond his reach, other things don't matter very much."

At the sight of the weary discontent on his handsome face, her heart softened, and as they stopped before the little cabin, which was their destination, she said kindly:

"Come in and see Uncle Mose with me, won't you?"

But the young man excused himself rather hurriedly, and delivering the basket into her hands he said good-morning, and walked rapidly back toward the town.

Margaret pushed open the door of the wretched little cabin, and just within sat Uncle Mose, engaged in his customary avocation of shoe-making, or to speak more accurately, shoe-mending. He was a spare and sinewy old negro, whose age, according to his own account, was "somewhar high up in de nineties." He was much bowed in figure, and lame in one leg.

Bushy tufts of dull gray hair rose on each side of his brown and polished crown, and his wrinkled and sunken cheeks were quite beardless. His expression was one of placid benevolence and contentment—a strange contrast to his surroundings. The room he occupied was hideously squalid and confused. The roof sloped in one direction and the floor in another, and the stove, which was unreasonably large, in a third. Old phials, suspended by their necks and partly filled with muddy liquids, decorated the walls, together with a pair of patched boots, a string of red peppers, several ears of pop-corn, and a leather-covered whipstock. In one corner hung a huge walking cane. Everything was thickly coated with dust.

The old man was seated near the perilously one-sided stove, in which a fire smoked and smouldered, though it was a balmy day, and in front of which a rusty old iron spade did duty for a door. His few old tools and pegs and twines were on a broken chair beside him.

When he looked up, over the top of his brass-rimmed spectacles, and saw who his visitor was, he broke into a broad smile of welcome, as he raised his withered old hand to his head in token of salutation.

"Dat you, missis?" he said. "What bin fetch you out dis time o' day? I is glad to see you, sho'. Come in, en take a seat."

He swept his tools and twines from the wooden seat to the floor, and rubbed the dusty surface several times with his hard palm. Margaret at once sat down, laying her long white draperies across her lap, to protect them from the dusty floor, showing a pair of neat little boots as she did so. Then she took off the cover of the basket, and revealed its contents to the old man's delighted gaze.

"Well, missis, to be sho'!" he exclaimed, his features relaxing in a grin of anticipative enjoyment, "Light bread, en chicken, en grapes! en what's dis, missis? Gemarna!* Whoo! How come you bin know so good what I done

* Blanc-mange.

bin hankerin' arter? I gwine tase a little, right now."

And using his shoemaking weapon as knife, fork and spoon indifferently, he fell to in earnest. He had probably been honest in his intention of only tasting a little, feeling it perhaps a lack of decorum to eat in the presence of his guest ; but once embarked on the alluring enterprise, he was in no humor to relax, and, uttering from time to time expressive ejaculations of enjoyment, he went on and on, until only the fruit remained. As he wiped his mouth on the back of his hand, he drew a long sigh of contented repletion.

" Dat wor good, sure 'nuff, missis," he said. "White folks' vittles tase mighty chice to me now, I tell you."

" I'm glad you liked it, Unclo Mose," said Margaret. " But tell me—I always meant to ask you—where that immense stick came from. Did any one ever use it ? "

"What, dat air olo stick, missis? Why, bress you, honey, dat air olo stick wor ole mars'r's, whar he bin use ter take when he druv out in de kyarrge, arter he bin git so big en fat. Yes, missis; he bin put he han's on de top en res' he chin on 'em, en when I bin had ter git out'n de ole place, de bin gin it ter me fur a sort o' memorandum."

"You were mighty fond of your old master, weren't you, Uncle Mose?" asked Margaret.

"Ah, dat's a fac', missis—dat's a fac'. Ole mars'r war mighty good to us. De wor three hund'rd on us, en he wor de mars'r, en we had ter know it. He done bin gin he niggers mighty good chance, ole mars'r is. Ebery man bin had he pig en he chickens, en ole mars'r he buy de young chickens en de eggs, en pay us de market price fur 'em. Yes, missis."

"And what would you do with the money, Uncle Mose?" Margaret asked.

"Dress my wife, missis. Lor' yes, dress my wife, en Queen. Queen war my oldes' daughter; en if you b'lieve me, missis, I dress dem two niggers same as de done bin white. I bin lucky nigger all my life, missis. Ole mars'r wor good enough, en when he bin die en young Rawjer take de place, t'war mos' same as hebben. I duhno *how* come young Rawjer wor so mile, for all he par wor so blusterin'. You see ole mars'r he mighty quick en hot-heddy. He let out at you sometimes, en hawler 'twel you think he gwine tar you to pieces; but done you be skeered, missis; he ain' gwine hit you a lick. When de new overseers 'd come, ole mars'r he 'low de mus' keep us down en work us hard, but Lor' missis, he ain' mean it. He gwine watch mighty close nobody don' 'buse his niggers, en he giv 'em plenty good food to eat, and see it done bin cook right, too. De did'n have no plates en knives to eat with. No missis; but what dem niggers want long o' plates en knives? De ain' got no right to complain cause de ain' eat off'n chany. De needn't think ole mars'r gwine let em come sit down at his table long o' him, 'kus he worn' gwine do it, en he *did'n* do it. No, missis.

The old man's tone was one of vehement indorsement of his master's policy, that there could be no mistaking.

"Did you marry one of your own master's slaves, Uncle Mose?" asked Margaret, presently.

"No, missis," Uncle Mose responded blandly; "I marry a gal whar 'long to one Mr. *Fitz-hugh.* De war heap o' likely gals whar 'long to ole mars'r, some bright yaller, and some black ez coals, en some mos' white, but seem like I could'n make up my mine to marry air one on 'em. I dunno *what* make I could'n take to 'em, but 't'war no use! I bin sot my eyes on a tall black gal, over to Mars'r George *Fitz*hugh's, en ebery other Sad'dy ole mars'r lemme knock off early en go see her. She done bin younger'n me, some odd yeers, en I tell her I wor'n' gwine cheat 'er. I tell her she mought look roun' a while, 'fo' we bin settle de thing. So, eff you b'lieve me, missis, I bin wait on her three yeers, 'fo' she compose her mine to marry me."

"Well, and what became of her?" said Margaret, as he paused ruminatively.

" Arter 'bout fo' yeers, missis, she wor sole away, Liza wor," he said in tones as benign and free from resentment as ever. " Lor' me, missis, how well I mine dat day! I bin' come up from de fiel' like t'wor down datterway " (suiting the action to the word), " de paff run long by de cabin do' pretty much. It wor like it done bin dis pass Chewsdy dat I come up to de do', en Aun' Tetsy, she tell me she heer 'Liza done bin sole. I stop short like, en I say '*what?*' en she tell me agin, en say she bin heer'd de done fotch her down to town ter take her off in de drove. I struck out for de great-'us at dat, en I tell ole mars'r all 'bout it. ' Knock off work, Mose,' ole mars'r say, 'en go to town en see eff she's thar. 'T'ain' no use try ter keep her, but mebbe you can see her en de chillun onc't mo'. You kin take White-foot.' I prick up my yeers at dat, for White-foot war de fleetes' horse ole mars'r got. Lor', missis, I wish yer could 'a see dat filly. De ain' no sich hosses now. Her legs war clean en straight ez a poplar, en her coat ——"

2

"But, Uncle Mose, go on about 'Liza."

"'T'war no use, missis," he said, with a patient head-shake. "When I got to town I bin hurry to de jail to see eff de bin lodge de gang in dar, but de tell me 'Liza bin gone off wid de rest on 'em dat very mornin'."

He ceased speaking, and sat staring in front of him in a preoccupied and ruminative way, from which Margaret saw it would be necessary to recall him.

"Well—what else, Uncle Mose?" she said gently; "what finally became of your wife?"

"Which wife, missis?" he replied, rousing himself by an effort, and looking about him blankly; "I had three on 'em."

Margaret refrained from asking whether it had been a case of "trigamy," or whether they had been successive, and said:

"You were telling me about 'Liza's being sold away. Did you never see her again?"

"No, missis," the old man answered gently. "I never see 'Liza no mo'. I see a man whar met her on de road, en he say she bin had de baby in her arms, walkin' 'long wid de gang, en de t'other chile wor in de cart wid de balance o' de chillun, en he say 'Liza busted out a-cryin', en 'low he mus' tell her ole man, eff we did 'n meet no mo' here b'low, she hope to meet in Hebben. En he ax her den whar she gwine ter, en she say she dunno, she think she bin heerd em say t'wor Alabammer; en dat's de las' word I ever heer o' 'Liza. Yes, missis."

Another meditative pause followed, and Margaret's sympathetic eyes could see that he was far back in the past.

"I bin had a daughter sole away, too, missis," he went on presently. "Yes, missis. She 'long to one Mr. Lane. He bin a hard mars'r, en he treated on her mighty bad, 'twel arter while she run off en went en put herself in jail. Yes, missis."

"How could she put herself in jail?"

"Dat how de do, missis. You see, when she bin run away, eff she done git caught, de have to put her in jail. So she jes' go en give herself up, en say she won' go back ter Mr. Lane,

—she be sole fust! So arter Mr. Lane fine out she one o' dat sort, he sole her. It so happen dat my brother Sawney wor gwine 'long de road, en she wor passin' in de cart, en she hawler out: 'Howdy, Unc' Sawney!' en Sawney say: 'Hi! who dat know me, en I don' know dem?' En she say: 'Lor' Unc' Sawney, don't you know Unc' Mose's Queen?' En Sawney say: 'Hi, Queen! Dat ain' you! Whar you gwine to?' En she say: 'I dunno, I ruther fer ter go ennywhere den to stay whar I done bin.' En I ain' never heerd o' Queen since."

At this point the old man was seized with a fit of coughing, which he made great efforts to repress, and fluently apologized for.

"You must excuse me, young missis," he said. "I bin cotch a bad cole, en it cough me all day en cough me all night, clar 'twel mornin'. I'se gettin' mighty ole en shacklin'. Yes, missis.

"De all been mighty good to me, missis," went on Uncle Mose, after a short pause, "from ole mars'r down. I hope to meet 'em all in Hebben. Ole mars'r ain' bin much fer religion in he life; but he die a mighty peaceful, happy death, en he forgive all he enemies. He bin kind en merciful, en I 'low de Lord 'll take him in. He always give his niggers heap o' religious encouragement, en when we bin go to de lick to be *babtize*, he bin gin us de fines' kind o' notes to de preacher, en eff you bin tell a lie or steal a chicken he ain' gwine say de fuss word 'bout it. Ef he come roun' to de cabin while we bin had meetin', he ain' gwine make no 'sturbance. He wait roun' 'twel we done sing de Doxoligum, en den he say what he come fer."

"Your religion has been a great comfort to you, Uncle Mose—hasn't it?" said Margaret, making an effort to keep back an irrepressible smile.

"Ah, dat's a fac', missis—dat's a fac', it has. Sometime it animate me very strong, en make me tower high 'bove de world; but den agin, sometime de very las' bit on it takes to flight, en ef you b'lieve me, missis, I ain' got no more religion den de palm o' your han'!"

"The greatest saints have complained of that, Uncle Mose," said Margaret; "it is one of the devil's strongest temptations."

"What, ole Sat'n, missis? Talk to me 'bout ole Sat'n! Don't I know him? You just give him de chance en he gwine fight you, mean enough!"

Margaret, much amused, was about to make a move to go, when Uncle Mose arrested her intention by saying:

"En so Mars' Rawjer got a little gal gwine git married. Well, well, well! Is I ever bin tell you, missis, 'bout de time I whip young Rawjer? Ha! ha! ha! I tell you, missis, I whale him good. He make me mad one day, 'bout ketchin de white folks' hosses, en I break me a little sprout, whar sprung up 'side a ole stump, in de very fiel' I help to clar forty yeers ago, en I warm he jacket fer him, good fashion. I mighty feared he gwine tell he par, but arter I git up by de stable, I does take my han' en slap it 'gin de stone fence, en one de little white boys say, 'I tell you, Uncle Mose kin hit hard'; en I say 'Ah, dat I kin, chile; dat's a fac;' en eff you b'lieve me, I skeered dat chile so bad, he ain' never tell he par yit;" and Uncle Mose went off into a long chuckle of delight. "When he bin git married en bring he wife home, we all went up to de house to see 'em, en drink de healths, en he tell de young missis this war Mose whar bin gin him that air whippin' he bin tole her 'bout. She war mighty pretty little thing, wid yaller hair en great big sof' blue eyes, en a little han' ez sof' en white ez snow. I was mos' feared to ketch hold on it, wid my ole black paw, but she would shake han's wid me, en she 'lowed maybe t'wor dat whippin' what make her husman sich a good man, en Mars' Rawjer he look at her fit to eat her up. She bin use ter gin out to de han's, arter she come, but Aun' Kitty she tote de smoke-'us key."

As Margaret rose to take leave, the old man rose also.

"I mighty proud'n dat dinner you bin fotch me, missis," he said. "Give my 'spects to yo' par en mar, en call agin, missis." And he lifted his cap and bowed her out with punctilious politeness.

As Margaret took her way homeward from the old negro's cabin, she was conscious of a more than usual softness in her heart for Uncle Mose and his reminiscences, and all the customs and traditions of which he was the exponent. Even Charley Somers seemed less reprehensible than he had been an hour ago, for the old man's talk had brought before her mind a system of things of which the inertia and irresponsibleness that jarred upon her so, in the people around her, seemed the logical outgrowth. She had often been told that her father, when a small boy, had been every day drawn to and from his school in a diminutive coach pulled by ten little negroes; and a number of similar anecdotes which she could recall gave her an insight into the absolute difference between that *régime* and the present, that made her somewhat ashamed of her intolerance, and mollified considerably her feeling toward young Somers, whom she determined to serve more kindly at their next interview. She was prompted further to this resolve by the fact that she had something to break to the young man, which she feared would go rather hard with him.

An opportunity which she had often longed for, to see the great world beyond her own section of country, and observe the manners and habits of men and women whose circumstances and traditions were directly opposed to her own, had been offered recently by a letter, received from a cousin who had married an army officer and was living in Washington, which conveyed an invitation for her to make her a visit. Her father and mother highly approved the plan and it seemed settled that she was to go, and while she longed for the new experience, she found her thoughts dwelling rather tenderly on the dear old home and friends, of whom, it seemed to her now, she had been ungratefully impatient.

CHAPTER II.

A FEW weeks later, Miss Trevennon found herself domesticated in her cousin's house in Washington, with surroundings so unfamiliar and circumstances so new to her that she found something to excite her interest and surprise almost every hour in the day. The perfect appointments of the house, which was gotten up with all the appliances of modern art, delighted and diverted her at every turn. "The mud-scraper," she wrote her mother, in her first letter home, "is a thing of beauty, and the coal-scuttle a joy forever."

There were no children in the family, which consisted only of General and Mrs. Gaston and a bachelor brother of the former, who made his home with them, although a large portion of his time was spent in New York. Margaret had already been an inmate of the house for ten days, and as yet had not seen him. Mrs.

Gaston, however, informed her that he might
appear at any moment, his trips to and from
New York being too frequent to entail the for-
mality of announcing himself.

Mrs. Gaston was a very clever and agreeable
woman and pretended, with some reason, to
know the world. Her marriage had been considered quite a brilliant one, as General Gaston's position, both social and official, was extremely good, and he had quite a large private
fortune in addition to his pay. He was not
so clever as his wife, but more thoughtful and
perhaps more sincere. It was a successful
marriage, and the Gaston establishment was
tasteful and well ordered. Mrs. Gaston, whose
health was indifferent, kept her room a good
deal when she could escape the exactions of
society, which she never allowed herself to
shirk; and her husband was so much absorbed
in his official and social duties that Margaret
was often alone.

"I am afraid you are frequently dull, my
dear," Mrs. Gaston said to her cousin one

morning, as the latter sat beside her couch in the little dressing-room where the invalid was taking her breakfast. "It will be brighter for you when the season fairly opens; but I purposely begged you to come now, so that we might have time to make acquaintance while we are quiet. I wish Louis would come home, but there's never any counting on him, he's so frightfully busy all the time. I never saw a man work so hard in my life."

Margaret looked a little puzzled: "I thought you told me—— " she began,

"That he is well off? So he is. He has quite a nice little fortune and there's no earthly reason why he should work so hard, except that he likes it; and from that point of view I don't blame him. 'Pleasure the way you like it,' is an axiom for which I have a profound respect, and Louis undoubtedly finds his chief pleasure in application to his profession."

"What is his profession?" Margaret asked; for, although it was evident that Mrs. Gaston was very fond of her brother-in-law, she had, for some reason, said very little about him to her cousin.

"He's an architect—I thought you knew—Ames & Gaston. Have you never heard of them?"

"No," said Margaret, shaking her head and smiling, "but that does not go for much. I am finding out that I have never heard of most things."

"It's really quite delightful that you never heard of Ames & Gaston," said Cousin Eugenia, laughing. "I shall inform Louis promptly, though he won't believe it, or if he does he'll set it down to the obtuseness of Southern people—a foregone conclusion in his mind! I must tell you that I anticipate some pleasure in seeing you enlighten him on that score."

" I am afraid I shall not be able to do much," said Margaret. "I do feel myself extremely ignorant by the side of General Gaston and yourself, especially when you talk of modern literature and art and music."

"You need not, I assure you. We are neither

of us more than ' cleverly smattered' on these subjects. Edward knows more than I do, though every one, himself included, believes the contrary. It's quite another thing with Louis, however ; he's a swell at that sort of thing, and is really thorough, and yet, do you know, I sometimes manage to impose on him immensely and make him think I've penetrated to the very root and fibre of a matter, when in reality I have only the most superficial knowledge of it ? But all this is a digression. There was something I wanted to say to you. It was about Edward's people. You know about the Gastons, I suppose ?"

Margaret looked slightly puzzled. "What do you mean ?" she said.

"Oh! I mean about their name and history and family traditions. It's an old Puritan family and one of the most illustrious in New England. I read somewhere the other day, that it was one of the few really historical families in America, and I have no desire to speak disrespectfully of them, only I do think they

make an unnecessary amount of fuss with themselves. Oh! I *must* tell you about my first
interview with Mr. Alexander M. Gaston. You
know who he is!"

"Really, I do not," said Margaret, lifting her
eyebrows with a deprecating smile.

"Well, you *are* green! but, however, it's unnecessary to enlighten you now, except to say
that he is Edward's uncle, and the head of the
great house of Gaston. He's been governor
and senator and foreign minister and all sorts
of things, and is now one of the most eminent
men in New England, and a very excellent and
accomplished gentleman. Well, soon after I
became engaged to Edward he came to call
upon me, and I must say his whole manner
and attitude toward me were rather amazing.
He was good enough to say that he welcomed
me into the family, but he took pains to intimate that I was about to be the recipient of
a great honor. The Gastons, he explained,
had been for centuries leaders of public thought
and opinion in their own State, and he was

obliging enough to supply me with the dates of the landing in New England of the founders of the house, and to dwell upon their prominence among the early Puritans. I listened respectfully to this tirade, and by the time it came to a conclusion I had my little speech ready, and when he took my hand and formally welcomed me into the great house of Gaston, I replied by saying that I knew it ought to be a source of much satisfaction to Edward and myself that we were, in our small way, doing something toward healing an old breach. 'My ancestors were Cavaliers,' I said, 'and for a Cavalier to marry a Puritan, is, even at this late day, helping at least a little to wipe out the memory of a long-standing feud.' Now, I flatter myself that was rather neat."

" Oh, Cousin Eugenia, how perfectly delicious !" exclaimed Margaret, with an outburst of gay laughter. "And what did he say ?"

"I don't exactly remember, my dear, but it was something clever and adroit. I know he retired very gracefully, and bore me no malice.

He has been very kind to me always, and I am said to be his favorite of all his nephews' wives. He is really a dear old boy, and quite worthy of all the adulation he receives, if only they wouldn't put it on the ground of ancestry. Why, the founder of the family was engaged in some sort of haberdashery business in London! It's odd, the inconsistencies one meets with! But I'm inured to it all now, and have learned to pose as a Gaston, like the rest of them! But what I wanted particularly to tell you, and what it concerns you to know is, that the Gastons—Edward and Louis as well as the others—are greatly prejudiced against Southerners. That was one reason why I asked you here."

"It may make matters very difficult for me," said Margaret, smiling.

"Not in the least, my dear. You have only to be yourself, assuming nothing. I feel a delightful security in letting matters take their course. You will know perfectly what to do, and I think nothing could be more inspiring

3

than forcing people to abandon foolish prejudices. I should not be sorry to have your
chance myself."

"Surely, the same opportunity must once
have been yours."

"Oh no, they won't accord me that for a
moment. They say, with truth, that merely to
have been born in the South does not make
me a Southerner, and that, having spent as
much time in the North—and, for that matter,
the East and West—as in the South, I must be
set down as a cosmopolitan."

"I am almost surprised to hear you say they
are prejudiced," said Margaret; "I should
suppose they were too intelligent for that."

"Just what I've always said. For my part,
I haven't an atom of prejudice in my composi-
tion. It is unworthy of enlightened human
beings, and so I tell Edward and Louis."

"And what do they say?"

"Oh, that they are not prejudiced, of course.
Denial is the only answer such people can
give. But, for all that, they are. I think

Northern people, as a rule, are more prejudiced than Southerners."

"They must go great lengths, if they are," said Margaret ; " but I am not speaking of the more enlightened ones, and I have always supposed that the existence of such feelings in Bassett was due to the fact that it is such a small place, and so shut off from contact with the world. And then, too, I think much of it is to be attributed to the fact that those poor people suffered so terribly by the war."

" Exactly. I often tell Edward and Louis that they are so much less justifiable, because they were the victors. I'm sure *I* feel it a very easy thing to be magnanimous toward a person I've got the better of. But I've long since ceased to apply arguments to a prejudice. Finding they did not answer, I thought a practical illustration might."

A moment's silence ensued, which Margaret presently broke by saying :

" Is Mr. Louis Gaston younger or older than your husband ? "

"Younger, of course,—years younger.   He's not quite thirty."

"Is he a bachelor or a widower?"

"A bachelor, of course.   Fancy Louis being a widower!   He stands on the high vantage-ground of lofty impregnability.   He is not in love, and he would fain have it believed he never has been, or at least only in a careless and off-hand manner.   Not that he avoids women. On the contrary, he goes into society, and enjoys it very much when he has time, which is not very often."

"Do you mean that he works out of office hours?"

"He has no particular office hours, and he works at all times, early and late.   His partner lives in New York and he is there a great deal, and there most of the work is done; but he is always drawing plans and making estimates here at home, and has a branch office down the street.   Sometimes he works in his room, and sometimes I persuade him to bring his designs down into the library, when there seems a likelihood of our having a quiet evening. I pretend I'm interested in them, to please him,—he does a great deal to please me; but I'm not so, really."

"They must be interesting to him, at any rate, to absorb him so completely."

"I should think so! Why, I've known Louis, when there was a stress of work, to sit up the entire night, and then take a cold bath and come down to breakfast perfectly fresh, and be ready afterward to go off down town and be at it again until night. It's enough to make one yawn to think of it."

Mrs. Gaston, suiting the action to the word, was settling herself more comfortably among the pillows, and so failed to observe the look of eager interest her words had called up in her companion's face. She had just arranged her position to her satisfaction, and turned to continue the conversation, when a quick step was heard ascending the staircase.

"That's Louis' step," she said suddenly.

"Close the door, please; he will probably stop to speak to me."

Margaret obeyed in silence, and the next moment the footsteps stopped at the door, and a very pleasantly modulated voice said:

"Any admittance to a repentant renegade, who comes to make his peace?"

"No," said Mrs. Gaston, quietly; "I'm not well—worse than usual, indeed—used up with recent exertions and in no mood to show clemency to offenders."

"And pray, in what have the recent exertions consisted?" the voice replied.

"Oh, the usual round of wearing domestic affairs, with a new item added."

"Ahem!" exclaimed the voice; " it would seem the young Southerner has arrived. Is it so?"

"Yes," said Mrs. Gaston, dryly, "she has."

"If I were not too generous, I should say, 'I told you so,'" went on the voice. "I have observed that Southern importations into

Northern climates are usually attended with certain disadvantages."

"Oh, she's a very nice little thing," said Mrs. Gaston, carelessly, "I think something can be made of her."

"And you are to have the pleasure of conducting the process of development, and Edward and I that of looking on at it—is that it? Where is she, by-the-way? Is there any danger of one's meeting her on the stairs, and having to account for one's self? A civilized man, encountered unexpectedly, might unsteady the nerves of the Importation—might he not?"

"Possibly," said Mrs. Gaston; "but there's no danger. I've given her a room far away from yours; so you will still have the privilege of keeping unearthly hours without disturbing any one."

"Thank you; that's very considerate; but I must be off. I want to get some papers from my room, and then I must go to keep an appointment."

"Of course! I shouldn't know you if you hadn't an appointment. It wouldn't be you. Go on; but be prompt at dinner."

"You may count upon me. And, by-the-way, you'll let me know whenever you'd like me to do anything for your young friend's entertainment. I shall not be likely to know the tastes and predilections of the Importation, but if you think of anything I can do, I am at your service."

"Thank you; but I let her look after herself pretty much. I fancy there will be no occasion to call on you."

She threw an amount of careless weariness into her voice as she said this, that contrasted strongly with the smile of unmixed amusement with which she turned her eyes on Margaret a moment afterward, as the footsteps outside were heard ascending the staircase.

"Well," she said quietly, "that's Louis. What do you think of him?"

"How can I possibly say?" said Margaret, divided between amusement and indignation.

"Surely you must have some impression of him," Mrs. Gaston urged.

"He has a very pleasant voice."

"You couldn't fail to notice that. I was sure you would. New Englanders are some-what maligned in the matter of voices, I think. That dreadful nasal twang, where it exists at all among the more cultivated, usually belongs to the women ; though I must say Edward has some relations, male and female, who set my teeth on edge whenever they come near me. But a really beautiful voice, such as Louis', is a rarity anywhere, and he pronounces his words so exquisitely! Only to hear him say 'Matthew Arnold' rests every bone in one's body. I dare say you would have expected to hear the endless succession of double o's, always attributed to *Noo* Englanders!"

"Oh, no!" said Margaret. "I always sup-posed cultivated New Englanders quite supe-rior to that."

"They suppose themselves to be so, also," said Cousin Eugenia ; "but they are not in all cases, by any means. Edward himself had a decided tendency in that direction when I married him. I have often told him that what first suggested to me to accept him was a curiosity to see whether he would address me as 'Oogenia,' when he grew sentimental; and I protest he did!"

Margaret could not help laughing at this, but she soon became grave again, and said seriously:

"I am afraid I must be rather a *bête noir* to Mr. Gaston."

"It would seem so," said Cousin Eugenia.

"I hope you will never call upon him to escort me anywhere, or do anything whatever for my entertainment," Margaret continued. "I wish you would promise me not to."

"With all my heart. I promise it as solemnly and bindingly as you like."

At this point the footsteps were heard returning down the stairs, and again they paused outside.

"Can you come and take this?" the pleasant voice called softly.

"Open the door and hand it through a little crack," Mrs. Gaston answered.

The knob was turned from without, and the door pushed open just wide enough to admit the entrance of a neatly done-up parcel, held in a large, finely formed hand.

Mrs. Gaston motioned to Margaret, who sat just behind the door, to take the parcel, and, not daring to protest, the girl moved forward and received it.

"Shake hands, in token of pardon for my slurs at the Importation," the voice said, in a tone of quiet amusement, and Margaret, obeying another peremptory nod and glance from Mrs. Gaston, transferred the parcel to her left hand, and put her right one for a moment into that of Louis Gaston.

"I perceive that the toilet is indeed in its initial stages," he said, "not a ring in place as yet! I hardly seem to know your hand in its present unfettered condition. I even think it seems slighter and colder than usual. The Importation must have taken a good deal out of you already."

Not choosing to have her hand imprisoned longer in that firm and friendly clasp, Margaret forcibly withdrew it and stepped back, while Mrs. Gaston said, naturally:

"Cease your invidious remarks and go to your appointment, Louis. Thank you for the candy."

The door was immediately closed from without, and again the footsteps retreated.

"I am glad you've shaken hands with Louis," Mrs. Gaston said; "it's an initiation to a friendship between you, and, in the end, you and Louis must be friends, though there will be certain inevitable obstructions at first. He is really the best and dearest creature that ever lived. He had a dreadful illness once from studying too hard for his college examinations, and Edward and I nursed him through it, and you don't know how we did yearn over that boy! He's been devoted to me ever since, one proof of which is, that he always brings me this candy from New York. Have some. I'm sure he ought to be good to me," she said, critically peering into the box from which Margaret had just helped herself, and selecting a plump chocolate drop ; " I certainly spoil him sufficiently. Still, there isn't very much one can do for a man like that. He has such frugal habits, it's quite baffling. But tell me what you think of him, after a second encounter."

" Why, nothing more than I thought before, except that he has a beautiful hand."

" Margaret, you are never disappointing," said Cousin Eugenia, warmly. "I felt sure you would observe that. Go now and write the letters that you spoke of while I dress, and then we'll go for a drive before lunch. And, by-the-way, while I think of it, put on your long black dress this evening, and wear the black lace at the throat and hands, as you had it the evening that the Kents were here. Don't wear any color, not even a bit of gold.

You know you gave me leave to make suggestions when you came, and it's the first time
I've used my privilege, though I think I am
usually rather fond of suggesting. Ring for
Lucy, please, and then hurry through your
letters, that we may have a nice long drive."

CHAPTER III.

A FEW minutes before six o'clock that evening, Margaret, clad in a long black gown that swathed her up to her milk-white throat, came slowly down the broad staircase of General Gaston's house and entered the empty drawing-room.

Finding herself alone, she moved across the warm, bright room to the table which stood under the chandelier, and taking up the evening paper, which had just been brought in, she began rather listlessly to run her eyes along its columns. Presently some particular item caught her attention, and so absorbed her that she was unconscious of approaching footsteps, until she caught sight of a gentleman who was just entering the room from the hall.

Lowering the paper, she waited for him to come forward, which he did with a certain perplexity of expression and a slight confusion of manner. Seeing these indications, the girl looked into his face with frank self-possession, and said gently:

"Miss Trevennon."

As there was no immediate response, she presently added:

"You are Mr. Gaston?"

The sound of his own name recalled him, and he came up and greeted her with a perfect ease that instantly put to flight the moment's confusion; not however, before a watchful eye, applied to a crack between the folding-doors of the library, had noted the fact of its existence. These doors were now suddenly thrown apart, and Mrs. Gaston, dressed in a gay and ornate costume, entered the room.

"I beg pardon of you both for not having been on hand to introduce you," she said, with careless composure, as she took her brother-in-law's hand and turned her cheek to receive his light kiss. "You have managed to dispense with my offices, I'm glad to see! How are you, Louis?—though it is the merest form to ask.

He is one of the hopelessly healthy people, Margaret, who are the most exasperating class on earth to me. Anything in the *Star*, dear? Let me see."

She took the paper from Miss Trevennon's hand, and began carelessly looking it over. Suddenly her eye lighted.

"Here's something that may interest you, Louis," she said, handing him the paper, as she pointed with her heavily jewelled finger to a paragraph headed :

"Southern Imports."

At the same instant General Gaston entered the room, and just afterward a servant announced dinner.

Mrs. Gaston had mentioned that it was characteristic of her to be a magnanimous victor, and it may have been that fact which prompted her great urbanity to her brother-in-law on the present occasion. She ran her hand through his arm affectionately, as she walked toward the dining-room beside him, and thanked him with great effusiveness for the delicious candy.

To all which he answered by the not very relevant response, uttered half under his breath :

"Never mind, madam! I'll settle with you for this."

Margaret, of course, was *vis-à-vis* to Louis Gaston at the table, and while both joined in the general conversation which ensued, she perceived, by her quick glances, that he was a man of not more than medium height, with a straight and well-carried figure and a dark-skinned, intelligent face. He had dark eyes, which were at once keen and thoughtful, and very white teeth under his brown mustache. Although in undoubted possession of these good points, she did not set him down as a handsome man, though his natural advantages were enhanced by the fact that he was dressed with the most scrupulous neatness in every detail, the very cut of his short dark hair, parted straight in the middle, and brushed smoothly down on top of his noticeably fine head, and the well-kept appearance of his rather long finger-nails, giving evidence of the fact that his toilet was performed with punctilious care.

It was something very new, and at the same time very pleasant to Margaret, to observe these little points in a person whose first and strongest impression upon her had been that of genuine manliness. In Bassett, the young men allowed their hair to grow rather long and uneven; and when, for some great occasion, they would pay a visit to the barber, the shorn and cropped appearance they presented afterward was so transforming as to make it necessary for their friends to look twice to be sure of their identity. As to their nails, in many instances these were kept in check by means of certain implements provided by nature for purposes of ruthless demolition, and when this was not the case they were left to work their own destruction, or else hurriedly disposed of in the intervals of vehement stick-whittling. Not a man of them but would have set it down as effeminate to manifest the scrupulous care in dress which was observable in Louis Gaston, and it was upon this very point that Margaret was reflecting when Gaston's voice recalled her.

"I'm uncommonly glad to get home, Eugenia," he said, tasting his wine, as the servant was removing his soup-plate. "I think Ames is beginning to find out that this Washington office is a mere subterfuge of mine, and that the real obstacle to my settling down in New York is my fondness for the domestic circle. I really wish Edward could manage to get sent to Governor's Island. I must confess I should prefer New York as a residence, if I could be accompanied by my household gods and my tribe. Shouldn't you, Miss Trevennon?"

Margaret had been sitting quite silent for some time, and Gaston, observing this, purposely drew her into the conversation, a thing his sister-in-law would never have done, for the reason that she had observed that her young cousin possessed the not very common charm of listening and looking on with a perfect grace.

"I have never been to New York," said Margaret, in answer to this direct appeal, "and I have only a limited idea of its advantages as a place of residence, though I don't doubt they are very great."

"They are, indeed," said Louis, observing her with a furtive scrutiny across the graceful mass of bloom and leafage in the *épergne.* "You will like it immensely."

"If I ever make its acquaintance," said Margaret, smiling. "Washington seemed to me the border-land of the Antipodes before I came here, and I have never thought of going beyond it."

"You have lived, then, altogether in the South?" said Gaston, with a tinge of incredulity in his voice, so faint as to escape Margaret, but perfectly evident to Mrs. Gaston, for the reason, perhaps, that she was listening for it.

"Yes, altogether," Margaret answered.

"My poor little cousin is in a most benighted condition," Mrs. Gaston said. "She has not only never been to New York, but—only think!—until to-day she never heard of Ames & Gaston!"

"Impossible! Unbelievable!" said Louis. "Was it for this that they designed 'All Saints,' and have even been mentioned in connection with the new skating-rink? Eugenia, you are a true friend. It will not be necessary for me to carry a slave about with me to remind me that I am a man, like the great monarch we read of in history; a sister-in-law is a capital substitute and performs her office quite as faithfully."

"Perhaps it is well for me," said Margaret, smiling demurely, "that I began my list of ignorances with such an imposing one; it will make those that follow seem trivial by comparison."

"There is wisdom in what you say, Miss Trevennon," said Louis; "and if you wish to impress yourself with the magnitude of the present one, get Eugenia to take you to see 'All Saints.'"

The conversation now turned into other channels, and it was not until Margaret was saying good-night to Mrs. Gaston, in the latter's dressing-room, that she reverted to this subject.

"I can well believe that Mr. Gaston is a clever architect," she said, "his eye is so keen and steady. I should like to see some of his work. This 'All Saints' Church is very beautiful, I suppose. Shall we really go to see it some day?"

Mrs. Gaston broke into her little light laugh.

"That's a piece of nonsense of Louis', my dear," she said. "It's a cheap little mission chapel, built by a very poor congregation in a wretched part of the town. The Travers girls got Louis interested in it, and he made them the designs and estimates and superintends its erection. Of course he charged them nothing; in fact, I believe he subscribed a good deal toward it himself. He is amused at the idea of their calling it 'All Saints,' and making it such a comprehensive memorial. He and his partner have designed some really beautiful buildings here, however, which I will show you.   Louis is very clever, don't you think so?"

"I hardly feel able to judge, yet," said Margaret, "but if you say so, I will believe it, for since I've been with you, Cousin Eugenia, I begin to think I never knew any one before who was clever."

"Why are you always forcing one to remind you of your ignorance, child?" retorted Mrs. Gaston, laughing lightly. "This is the most convincing proof we have had of it yet."

As Margaret went up to say good-night, she felt a strong impulse to express some of the ever-ready affection which her cousin's kindness had awakened in her heart; but Cousin Eugenia was a woman to whom it was very hard to be affectionate, and she thwarted her young cousin's intention now by turning her cheek so coolly that the ardent words died on the girl's lips.   Mrs. Gaston was naturally unsympathetic, and it almost seemed as if she cultivated the quality.   However that might be, it was certain that, at the end of a month

spent in daily companionship with this bright
and agreeable cousin, Margaret was obliged to
admit to herself that she had not taken one step
toward the intimate friendship she would have
liked to establish between them. Her cousin
was kindness itself, and always companionable
and agreeable, but she was scarcely ever really
serious, although she had at hand a reserve of
decorous gravity which she could always draw
upon when occasion required.

CHAPTER IV.

"EUGENIA," said Louis Gaston, tapping at his sister-in-law's door one morning, "I stopped to say that I will get tickets for Miss Trevennon and yourself for the opera Monday evening, if you say so."

"*I* don't say so, my dear Louis, I assure you," returned Mrs. Gaston opening her door and appearing before him in a tasteful morning toilet. "If you take Margaret and me to the opera, it must be for your own pleasure; she is not the kind of guest to hang heavily on her hostess' hands. I've never been at a loss for her entertainment for a moment since she has been here, and what is more, scarcely ever for my own. I find myself quite equal to the task of providing for her amusement, and so it has not been difficult for me to keep my promise of not calling upon you in her behalf."

"You certainly never made me any such

promise as that, and it would have been very absurd if you had."

" Ah, perhaps then it was to Margaret that I made it! The main point is that I've kept it."

" Of course, Eugenia, it goes without saying, that when you have a young guest in the house my services are at your disposal."

" Oh, certainly. Only, in this instance, I prefer to let all suggestions come from yourself. I know you only put up with my Southern relatives because of your regard for me, and, strong as is my faith in that sentiment, I don't want to test it too severely ; but I won't detain you. Mrs. Gaston and Miss Trevennon accept with pleasure Mr. Gaston's kind invitation for Monday evening. The opera is *Favorita*—isn't it ? Margaret has never heard it, I know; it will be very nice to initiate her. Will you be at home to dinner to-day ? "

" Yes, of course," replied the young man, looking back over his shoulder as he walked away.

"Oh, of course!" soliloquized his sister-in-law, as she turned back into her apartment. "Quite as if you were never known to do otherwise! Oh, the men! How facile they are! Louis, as well as the rest! I had expected something to come of this case of propinquity, but I did *not* expect it to come so quickly. He hasn't dined out more than twice since she's been here, and then with visible reluctance, and he has only been once to New York, and I suspect the designs are suffering. And Margaret too! It's quite the same with her—saying to me last night that his manners are so fine that she is constrained to admit that, taking Louis as an exponent of the Northern system, it must be better than the one she had always supposed to be the best! It works rapidly both ways, but there must be a hitch before long, for in reality they are as far asunder as the poles. Every tradition and every prejudice of each is diametrically opposed to the other. How *will* it end, I wonder?"

It happened that Mrs. Gaston did an unusual

amount of shopping and visiting that day, and was so fatigued in consequence that she had dinner served to her in her own apartment, and Margaret dined alone with the two gentlemen. Afterward she went up and spent an hour with the vivacious invalid, whom she found lying on the bed, surrounded by an array of paper novels by miscellaneous authors, the titles of which were of such a flashy and trashy order that Margaret felt sure she would never have cared to turn the first page of any of them, and wondered much that her intelligent and cultivated cousin could find the least interest in their contents. Mrs. Gaston was in the habit of ridiculing these novels herself, but would say, with a laugh, that they were " the greatest rest to her," and Margaret was continually expecting to find her immersed in some abstruse work, which would sufficiently tax her mental powers to account for the liberal allowance of relaxation which was to counteract it ; but, so far, she had been disappointed.

Mrs. Gaston laid her novel by on Margaret's

entrance, and gave her young cousin a cordial welcome. The two sat talking busily until General Gaston came up to his dressing-room to prepare for a lecture to which he was going, and to which he offered to take Margaret. His wife put her veto on that plan, however, pronouncing it a stupid affair, and saying that Margaret would be better entertained at home.

"But you are not to stay up here with me, my dear," she said. "Go down stairs. Some one will be coming in by-and-by, I dare say, and you must not think of coming back to entertain me. I am bent on seeing how this absurd story ends; it's the most deliciously preposterous thing I ever read,—so bad, that it's good! Say good-night now, dear. I know you are never dull; so I dismiss you to your own devices. I don't know where Louis is, but he may come and join you after a while. There's never much counting on him, however."

When Margaret descended to the drawing-room, the library doors were thrown apart, and through them she could see Louis Gaston bending over some large sheets of heavy paper, on which he was drawing lines by careful measurement. He looked up at the sound of her footsteps, and, as she took a magazine from the table, and seated herself in a large chair before the fire, he came in with his pencil in his hand, and leaning his back against the end of the mantel, said :

"Eugenia tells me you have never seen *Favorita*, and I so rejoiced to put an end to that state of affairs! You don't know what an absolute refreshment it has been to me to observe your enjoyment of the music you have heard since you have been here. I don't think I have ever received from any one such an impression of a true appreciation of music. It seems rather odd, as you neither play nor sing yourself."

"It pleases me to think that my own incapacity does not interfere in the least with my enjoyment of music," Margaret said. "When I hear beautiful music my pleasure in it is not impaired by any feeling of regret that

I cannot produce such a thing myself. It no more occurs to me to long for that, than to long to create a beautiful sunset when I see one."

"The fact that one is attainable, while the other is not, would make a difference, I think." He paused a moment, and then went on with his pleasant smile: "Do you know this discovery of mine—that of your fastidious appreciation of music—has been the thing that deterred me from inflicting any of my own upon you? I was so set against this that I made Eugenia promise not to acquaint you with the fact that I can sing a little."

"How could you do that?" exclaimed Margaret, reproachfully, with a keen conception of what lovely effects in singing might be produced by this richly modulated voice, whose spoken utterances she so admired. "I might have had such delight in hearing you sing! I am accustomed to having music so constantly at home. We have a friend there, a young man, who is almost like one of our own household, who sings beautifully. He has a lovely voice, so pure and strong, but entirely uncultivated. In some things it shows this almost painfully, but there are others that he renders exquisitely. Sacred music he sings best."

"Ah, that I have never tried, at least not much. Your friend's voice is the opposite of mine. I had really very little to begin with, and an immense deal of practice and training has not enabled me to do much more than direct properly the small amount of power I possess, and disguise its insufficiency more or less. It isn't very much, after all, and yet how I have pegged away at my scales and exercises! I had a most exacting master when I was in Germany, and as I was studying my profession at the same time, I wore myself almost to a skeleton. I studied very hard at the School of Architecture, but I never practised less than three hours a day—often four."

He was talking on, very lightly, but he stopped short, arrested by an expression on the face of his companion that he was at a loss

to account for.   There was a look of enthusi-
astic ardor in her eyes that amounted to positive emotion.

"How can you speak so lightly of a thing
that was really so noble?" she said, in a voice
full of feeling.

Louis' face broke into a smile of sheerest
astonishment, but at the same time he felt
himself strangely stirred by the feeling that he
had roused this warm admiration in the breast
of this fair young lady.

"My dear Miss Trevennon," he said earnestly, "you amaze me by applying such a
word to my conduct.   I went abroad to study
architecture and music, and there was every
reason why I should make the most of the
three years I had allotted to these purposes.
That I did my part with some degree of thor-
oughness was only what I felt bound to do, in
the simplest justice to myself and others.
When I think of the fellows who accomplished
twice what I did, contending against such ob-
stacles as poverty, or ill-health, or the absence

of proper facilities, I find the word *noble*, as applied to myself, almost humiliating. Do you know, your views on some points are extremely puzzling to me ? "

" I am at sea," said Margaret gently, with a hesitating little smile. " Things that I see about me seem strange and unfamiliar, and I often feel that I have lost my bearings. But your resolute application to studies that must often have been wearying and laborious, to the exclusion of the relaxations most young men find necessary, rouses my profound admiration. I have never known a man who was capable of a thing like that."

" Will you do me the kindness to tell me if I am blushing ? " said Louis. " I veritably believe so, and as it is a thing I have never been known to do before, I should like to have the occurrence certified to. I venture to hope, however, that the fact is accounted for by my being physically thick skinned, and not morally so, for I have known myself to be blushing when the fact would not have been suspected by outsiders. Just now, however, I fancy it must have been evident to the most casual observer."

He saw that the levity of his words and tones were, for some reason, discordant to Miss Trevennon, and so he spoke in a graver voice, as he said:

"I feel musical to-night, and almost as if I could overcome the hesitation I have spoken of sufficiently to sing you some of the music of *Favorita* in anticipation of Monday night."

"Oh, why don't you? It would be so delightful!" exclaimed Margaret, fired at the suggestion.

"I never feel that I can sing well when I have to play my own accompaniments," he said. "But for that——"

"Oh, if you have the music, do let me play for you!"

"Could you do it? I thought you did not play. Have you also been practising concealment?"

"My music amounts to nothing, but I could

easily manage an accompaniment. Have you the notes ? "

"Yes, just at hand. What a delightful idea! I never thought of this. You shouldn't have cheated me out of such a pleasure all this time. Let me open the piano. Come ! "

He tossed his pencil down upon the table, and moved across the room as he spoke. Seeing his action, Margaret checked herself as she was following, and said suddenly :

" I forgot your work. I really cannot interfere with that."

" Never mind the work. The work may go. I'll make it up somehow. Could you manage this, do you think ? "

By way of answer, Margaret seated herself and ran over the prelude with tolerable ease, and at the proper time nodded to him to begin.

There was no interruption until the really impressive voice had died away in the last note, and then Margaret dropped her hands on her lap and said, with a long-drawn breath :

" I can see no lack. It is most beautiful. I

think you must have greatly under-estimated your voice. It has a quality that touches me deeply."

"What there is of it does pretty well," Louis answered, smiling, well pleased at her earnest commendation. "Ames says I'm the best singer to have no voice that he ever heard, which is the greatest amount of praise I can lay claim to."

"I feel more than ever, now, the lack of cultivation in Mr. Somers' voice," said Margaret. "It is really a grand organ, but he scarcely knows how to sing anything with entire correctness, unless it is something in which he has been carefully drilled by some one who knows a little more than himself. I wish he could hear you sing."

"I wish I could hear him," said Louis. "If he has the voice, the cultivation can be acquired readily enough; but with me the utmost has been done. Much of this music is rather beyond me. Let us try a ballad."

He was bending over the rack, in search of

some particular piece, when the door-bell sounded. They both heard it, and their eyes met with a look of disappointment.

"It's too bad," said Margaret, regretfully. "I don't want to be interrupted."

"In that case," said Louis, promptly, arresting the servant on his way to the door by a quick motion of the hand, "suppose you allow me to have the ladies excused."

Margaret assented readily, and the order was accordingly given.

A moment later the servant came into the room, presenting two cards on a tray. Gaston glanced at them, and Margaret saw his face change slightly.

"I am afraid Eugenia will make me suffer for this," he said. "One of these visitors was young Leary."

"Who is he?" asked Margaret, simply.

"You surely know who the Learys are?" Gaston replied, in a tone of reproachful incredulity that was almost severe. "They come of one of the most distinguished families at the

North, and are here for the winter.   The father
of this young man has held various important
diplomatic and political offices. They visit very
little, and Eugenia will be annoyed that young
Leary has not been admitted. I don't think
he has ever called here before, except to
acknowledge an invitation. He sat near us at
the theatre the other night, and I saw that he
observed you ; so this visit is probably a tribute to you."

"I don't know that you have said anything
about him to make me regret him especially,"
said Margaret, "only that he's Mr. Leary ; and
what's in a name? Is there any reason why
one should particularly desire him as an acquaintance ? "

Mr. Gaston looked slightly bewildered.
Then he began to speak, and checked himself
suddenly. Then, turning back to the piano,
and beginning to look over the music, he said,
somewhat hurriedly :

"It is only that they are people it's well to
be civil to."

There was something in the tone Louis took, in regard to this matter, that puzzled Margaret —a tone that had also puzzled her in the other members of the Gaston family. There seemed to be a certain anxiety with all of them to know the right people, and be seen at the proper houses, and have only the best people at their own. Margaret Trevennon, for her part, had never had a qualm of this sort in her life, and supposed, moreover, that only vulgar or uncertainly posed people could possibly be subject to them. And yet here were people who were not only not vulgar but more elegant and charming than any men and women she had ever known, who were entitled to, and actually held, an unimpeachable social position, and who yet seemed to find it necessary to struggle hard to maintain it, and were continually possessed by a positive anxiety to appear to be distinguished! Really, it seemed their first and principal concern. This was the first time she had seen a decided indication of the feeling in Louis Gaston, and somehow

it hurt her more in him than in the others.
Unconsciously she gave a little sigh.

"Dear me!" she thought to herself, "what
an unpleasant idea! Why need people assume
anything, when they actually have it all? It
never occurred to me that really nice people
could give themselves any concern of this sort."

And then, as she turned and suddenly met
Louis' eyes, her face broke into a smile of sudden amusement.

"What is it?" said the young man, eagerly.

"I was laughing at some lines from the
'Bab Ballads' that happened to come into my
head just then," she said.

"What were they? I dote upon the Babs.
Do let's have them."

> "Lord Lardy would smile and observe,
>   'How strange are the customs of France!'"

quoted Margaret. "I dare say they don't
seem very relevant. But come, let's go on
with the music," she added, hurriedly. "We
must not prolong the interruption."

Mr. Gaston had smiled at her quotation and then become suddenly grave. As he selected a sheet of music and put it on the rack before her, he said seriously :

"I sometimes see that there are little points that we look at very differently. Perhaps we may come to understand each other by-and-by. I hope so, sincerely. And now, are you familiar with this, and do you care for it?"

The selection happened to be a favorite of Margaret's, and she entered delightedly into its rendition, and very soon the lovely strains of the sweet, sympathetic voice had banished all discordant thoughts and memories.

"There, Miss Trevennon," he said, as the song came to an end, "you've heard me do my little best now. Your accompaniments suit me perfectly. I am sure I never sang better. I hope we may have many another pleasant evening, such as this, together."

Margaret had risen from the piano and was standing before the fire, and she watched him with mingled interest and surprise, as he neatly replaced the music in the rack, lowered the instrument, and carefully arranged the cover, with a habit of orderliness of which she had also seen indications in General Gaston. It was to her almost a new trait, in men.

"Cousin Eugenia insists upon early hours, now that I am not going out," said Margaret, "so, as it is half-past ten, I will say good-night. I feel rather guilty," she added, pausing in the door-way, "for interrupting your work to-night. I dare say you wanted to finish it."

"Oh, as to that, it isn't a matter of choice," he murmured; "Ames must have those estimates to-morrow, and they are bound to go on the morning train."

"And when are they to be done?"

"Now, at once. I can easily finish them off to-night," he replied carelessly. "Pray don't look as if you had committed a mortal sin, Miss Trevennon," he added, smiling. "I assure you I don't weigh this little nocturnal application as dust in the balance against the pleasure

I've had in this musical evening with you. I hope it is not on my account you are hurrying off. I assure you there is abundance of time for my purposes. I shall take these papers to my room and finish them."

But Margaret, bent upon not hindering him further, retired at once.

The next morning Mrs. Gaston asked her brother-in-law at breakfast, whether he had not passed her room about sunrise, and, with some confusion, he was compelled to own that he had.

"What provoking ears you have, Eugenia!" he said; "I flattered myself that a mouse could not have been more noiseless. I am sorry to have disturbed you, especially as you had not been feeling well."

"Oh, I was awake, at any rate. But what was the occasion of your early expedition?" she asked, without showing any especial surprise.

"I had to post some papers to Ames," he said; "and though I had told Thomas I would ring for him to take them, the morning was so bright and clear that I fancied I should like the walk. And really it was most refreshing."

"I can fancy you needed refreshment," Mrs. Gaston said, "if, as I don't doubt, you had been at work all night."

Mr. Gaston made no response. He was helping himself from a dish offered by a servant at the moment, and seemed disposed to let the matter drop; but Margaret, urged by an irresistible impulse, arrested his eye and said quickly:

"Had you?"

"Had I what, Miss Trevennon?"

"Had you been at work all night?"

"Pretty much, I believe; but why do you look so tragic? I am not in delicate health, that the lack of a little sleep should entail serious consequences."

"'Pleasure the way you like it'!" said Mrs. Gaston. "Louis really likes that sort of thing; he deserves no credit for it. I used to apprehend that I should find myself brother-in-

law-less very shortly in consequence of those
habits, but he thrives on them ; he's the health-
iest person I know. Don't waste your sympathy on him, Margaret; keep it all for me. It
isn't those who endure hardships, but those
who can't endure them that should be pitied."

CHAPTER V.

THE season was now fairly opened, and Mrs. Gaston kept her young guest liberally supplied with amusement. There were all sorts of entertainments for them to go to, some of which Margaret found very inspiring and delightful, and some extremely dull. Cousin Eugenia, however, found nothing unprofitable. Every visit and every entertainment served some purpose, in her abstruse economy, and, if she failed to derive actual diversion from any, it still fulfilled some end, and in some manner was turned to account.

She would take Margaret with her on the endless round of afternoon calls that she made, never doubting that she was conferring an immense favor on her young country cousin, until the latter begged to be excused from some of them, confessing that they wearied her. This was a great surprise to Cousin Eugenia, who cherished the honest conviction that every opportunity of catching a glimpse of the great world of fashion must perforce be esteemed a high privilege and delight by this little Southern cousin, whom she pitied profoundly for her necessary isolation from such sources of happiness. Margaret was perfectly aware of this, and secretly much amused at it. That Cousin Eugenia, or any one, should commiserate her upon her lot in life was something very strange to her, for she had always known herself to be a very happy and fortunate girl.

"The Kellers give such stupid parties!" said Cousin Eugenia one evening, as she and Margaret were returning from a large entertainment. "I haven't missed one of them for the past five years, and they are asphyxiating affairs. I'm glad this one is well over."

"Why do you go to them, then?"

"Oh, every one does. At least every one who can. You saw how full the rooms were this evening, and yet every one there was bored."

6

"I was, undoubtedly," said Margaret, "and for that reason I should certainly not go again."

"You can afford to be independent, my dear, being here only on a visit, but if you lived in Washington you'd soon find that it was desirable for you to be seen at the Kellers'."

"Why?"

"Oh, because of their position."

Margaret was silent a moment, and then she said impulsively:

"Do excuse my asking such a thing, Cousin Eugenia, but I really want to understand. Could it possibly enhance your social value to be seen anywhere?"

Cousin Eugenia gave a little shrug.

"You put things so oddly, child, with your Southern notions! Of course our social position is fixed and definite and nobody would dispute it. But, large as the Kellers' circle is, their parties are very *recherché*, and it's well worth while to be seen there."

"I thought——" began Margaret.

"Well, go on," said her cousin, as the girl hesitated. "Out with it. Let me hear."

"I was only going to say that I thought a lady, born and reared, never had to think of anything like that."

"Like what?"

"Where she is seen and whether her associations will be considered correct. I thought that it would all come of itself—that a lady would not be in danger of making mistakes of that sort, because what she did would be the natural outgrowth of what she was."

"Those may be the Southern ideas, but you'd not find them to answer here."

"I don't know whether they are Southern ideas or not," said Margaret; "I never knew they were ideas at all. Certainly, I have never heard them formulated before, and I don't quite know how to express myself. They simply seem to me instincts."

"That's because of the associations you have had," said Mrs. Gaston. "I have seen very little of your parents of late years, but they have lived in my mind as people of thorough refinement. Your father is a model of a gentleman—the most high-bred man I ever knew, I think."

A radiant light came into Margaret's face.

"My darling, dear old father!" she said, fondly. "There is surely no one like him, and yet if I were to repeat your compliment to him, how amazed he would be! He has not an idea how fine he is, and has never once paused to consider whether he is high-bred or not. He would not hurt the feelings of the lowest wretch on earth—there is no one too mean for his kindly consideration. May I tell you an idea that has occurred to me, when I've been in society here, surrounded by such well-dressed, elegant looking, accomplished men, and have compared them to him? It is that they are all trying to be what he is."

Mrs. Gaston did not reply at once, but her silence proceeded from no feeling of intolerance of this sentiment. She was not at all given to resenting things, partly because of a natural indolence, and partly because she did not feel enough on any subject to be biassed by impulse.

" I can understand your having that feeling about your father," she said, presently, " and it's quite possible it may be true. We will submit the point when we find any one wise enough to decide it for us. But the world is large, and there are many men and many minds, and manners vary in different places. That line of tactics would not do in Washington."

At this point in their conversation they found themselves at home, and the subject was consequently dropped.

It happened about this time that some of Mrs. Gaston's wide circle of Southern connections, who were always cropping up in Washington, came to the city, and Cousin Eugenia took Margaret and went to call upon—or, as she did not hesitate to put it, to inspect them. They were a General and Mrs. Reardon, the former an ex-Confederate officer, who had been previously in the United States army, and who was distantly related to both Mrs. Gaston and Margaret, though neither of them had anything more than a slight acquaintance with him.

Margaret soon perceived that Cousin Eugenia did not consider them up to the mark socially—a fact which was further evidenced by their being invited to lunch, and not to dinner, next day. No one was asked to meet them, and Mrs. Gaston excused the gentlemen on the score of business hours. Margaret noted the whole proceeding, and saw through it and beyond it. Cousin Eugenia was perfectly polite and pleasant—extremely sweet, in fact—and yet there was something in her manner toward these simple Southern people, of a type so familiar to Margaret Trevennon, that the girl involuntarily resented. She showed none of this feeling to Mrs. Gaston, however, for she was beginning to understand that, although that clever lady in matters of abstract theory appeared to be most reasonable and open to

conviction, she was adamant itself in carrying out her peculiar designs and purposes,
and quite unused to interference from any
one.

The Reardons came next day, according to
appointment, and the little luncheon-party
passed off very pleasantly, greatly owing to
Margaret's efforts to make it do so.

When the guests were taking leave, they
asked if Mrs. Gaston and Margaret would not
go with them to an Art Exhibition in the evening. The proposal came, in a subdued and
deprecating sort of way, from Mrs. Reardon,
who was still young and pretty enough to be
somewhat eager for pleasure, and although
Mrs. Gaston declined it for herself, on the
score of indisposition, she encouraged Margaret to go, and the latter very willingly agreed
to do so.

She went accordingly, and was pretty well
entertained with what she saw, recognizing
some acquaintances, among whom was young
Mr. Leary, who had been sufficiently per-

severing to call again, with better success next time, and who had always been especially polite to Margaret on meeting her in society. Shortly before leaving, an acquaintance of General Reardon's came up, to whom Margaret was presented. He was a Major King, a Southern man, as Margaret somehow divined at a glance, and a resident of Washington, as it soon appeared. Before the party separated, he inquired where Miss Trevennon was staying, and asked her permission to call upon her. Margaret yielded the permission, of course, but with a strange feeling of reluctance ; she saw that, though a familiar type of Southern man, he was not a favorable one. There was a sort of aggressive self-confidence in his bearing, which was unpleasant enough to her, but which she knew would be positively offensive to the prejudiced minds of the Gastons. He belonged to a class she knew well—men whose range of vision had been limited, but who were possessed of a feeling of superiority to others in general, and an absolute conviction of superiority to the best Yankee that ever lived. It was an attitude of mind that had always irritated her, but she had never felt the force of it with such indignation as now, when she was being hourly impressed with the worth and superior qualities of these people whom her Southern compatriots regarded with such scorn. If Major King should come to call, however, she could feel confident that he would not betray the presence of this vindictive feeling, for, despite her disapproval of his tone and manner in general, she felt that she could count upon his possessing a spirit of courtesy, a hidden germ of which she had rarely found wanting in a Southern man's breast.

Margaret mentioned, at breakfast next morning, the fact of her having met Major King, and inquired of her friends if they knew him. The two gentlemen were silent, and Mrs. Gaston replied by a simple negative. She had intended to mention the fact that he had proposed to call upon her, but some instinct prevented her doing so. Very probably he would not come; and, besides, she had an indefinable feeling that there was danger in the topic.

It had become a habit with Margaret to go from the breakfast-table to the bow-window, on the corner of the house, to watch for the coming of the postman, and recently Mr. Gaston had fallen into the way of accompanying her. As the two young people found themselves together in the richly curtained recess, Margaret turned to her companion, with a smile, and said :

"Mr. Leary was there last night. He talked to me for quite half an hour. Ought I to have been elated?"

"Certainly not," replied the young man, frowning slightly. "Why do you ask such a thing? The idea is quite absurd."

"Yes, isn't it?" said Margaret, smiling. "He has so little sense, and he talks so much about himself. Here comes the postman!" She broke off suddenly, running to open the door herself, never divining that it would have been considered more decorous to wait until Thomas came up from the lower regions, and, with his usual deliberation, brought in the letters on his silver tray.

CHAPTER VI.

IT happened one evening, a few days later
on, that Margaret found herself once more
tête-à-tête with Louis Gaston. General and Mrs.
Gaston had gone to a dinner, from which Margaret was not sorry to be excused.

It was a cold and rainy evening in December,
and the drawing-room, with its rich drapery
and soft, deep Persian carpeting, was delight-
fully comfortable and warm, the wind, as it
whistled and blustered outside, adding to this
effect. The bright lights which hung from
the ceiling, together with the glowing fire in
the grate, shed a perfect wealth of warmth and
radiance around, and brought out the delicious
fragrance of the fresh flowers, which filled a
china bowl on a distant table. Louis, as on
the former occasion, bent over the table, just
within the library door, with his back toward the drawing-room, and Margaret, as

before, sat in the deep arm-chair before the fire.

"This is the lucky chance that I've been waiting for," said Gaston, turning to look at Margaret, as she settled herself with her book. "It is such a bad evening that I think we may hope for an immunity from visitors, and in a few minutes I shall lay by my work and come and try some new music I've provided, if you agree."

"I shall be charmed," said Margaret, with ready acquiescence. "I feel just in the humor for it. I utterly repel the proposition, however, if you are going to sit up all night in consequence."

"I will not, I assure you. It is not necessary, in the least. I'll just finish off a small bit that I am engaged on at present, and then put the rest by until to-morrow."

He returned to his work, and Margaret to her reading, and for a few moments the silence was unbroken, save by the sound of the wind and rain outside, and the soft little noises made by Louis with his pencil and rule.

Suddenly the door-bell rang, and, as before, they looked at each other regretfully. Louis was about to make the same proposition that his companion had responded to so promptly on the former occasion, but a look at Margaret's face checked him. An instinct which she scarcely understood herself, made it impossible for her to do a thing like that now. The fact that she was conscious of feeling a strong liking for Louis, restrained her from giving such a proof of it as this would be.

"I am sorry to give up the music," she said simply, as Thomas went by to the door, unchallenged. "There is still room to hope that it is a call that will not concern us."

For a moment this seemed likely, as there was a short colloquy with Thomas at the door before the visitor was admitted, and even after that he lingered to remove his overcoat and rubbers in the hall, with a deliberation that implied a degree of familiarity that Margaret could not identify as belonging to any visitor at the house whom she had yet met.

The next moment, as Louis Gaston and herself were both watching the door-way, Major King appeared, tall, gaunt, and awkward, but eminently self-possessed.

His loosely hung, impractically tall figure was clad in the inevitable shiny black "best clothes," that poor Margaret knew so well, even to the cut of the long frock-coat, with its flapping tails behind and its bagging, unhindered fronts, between which was displayed, through a premeditated opening in the vest, a modicum of white shirt-front, interrupted for an inch or so by the fastening of the upper buttons, only to reveal itself in more generous expansiveness higher up upon the Major's manly bosom.

Margaret's quick eye at once perceived the incongruity of the whole situation, and warned her of the necessity of effort on the part of all to reconcile and overcome it. She went forward and received Major King with the perfect politeness which was as natural to her as breathing, and then turned to present Mr.

Gaston, who, with the folding-doors of the library opened wide, was quite as if he were in the same room.

Gaston's aspect, at the first glance she gave him, was absolutely startling to her. His whole bearing had changed. He had risen from his seat and turned toward the drawing-room, and was standing by the table, very erect and still. The expression of his face was repellant to the last degree, the brows were contracted in a slight but perceptible frown, and the lips were shut with a firm severity.

Margaret, as she mechanically named the two men to each other, could not help drawing a swift mental contrast between the gaunt Southerner, whose features were, in reality, the handsomer of the two, and the Northern man, in his quiet evening dress, and wondering why the latter looked so greatly the superior. Mr. Gaston's attitude, despite its stiffness, was dignified and impressive, and Major King's, notwithstanding its ease, was slouching and ungainly.

But the most significant point of contrast came when each man, after his kind, acknowledged the introduction.

" Glad to meet you, sir," said Major King, in loud, reverberating tones, and made a motion forward, as if to extend his hand. This impulse was repressed, however, by the short, supercilious bow with which the other responded, pronouncing the two words, "Good-evening," with a chilling and clear-cut utterance that formed the strongest possible contrast to the stranger's bluff and off-hand style of address. Margaret observed that he did not pronounce Major King's name at all.

The young girl watched this interchange of greetings with a rush of conflicting emotions. Indignation, shame, astonishment and real pain fought for the predominance ; but above all, she was conscious of an instinct which made her feel that the Southern man's side was her side.

Mr. Gaston, as soon as the introduction was over, resumed his seat at the library-table,

7

and went on with his work, turning his back squarely toward the drawing-room, an action which made it impossible for Major King to fail to realize that he was being intentionally and deliberately slighted. How galling this knowledge must be to a Southern man Margaret well knew, and she felt all her sympathies enlisted for Major King. With the keenest anxiety she watched to see what his course would be.

With a slight flushing of the cheek and a dark flashing of the eye, the tall Southerner seated himself in a delicate little gilt chair, which he proceeded to tip backward, until his heavy weight caused the slight wood-work to creak ominously. Then, in response to a brilliant leader respecting the weather, thrown out by poor Margaret in her extremity, he launched into a fluent and somewhat irrelevant strain of conversation, which soon made it evident that he could go alone. His voice, alas! was loud and self-asserting, and his whole manner so arrogant and ill-bred that Margaret felt

her spirit of partisanship growing fainter and
fainter. One thing alone was clear to her, and
that was her own course. She heard Major
King with polite attention, and answered his
remarks, when his fluency would permit, with
entire courtesy. But Margaret was on the
rack the whole time as he talked on, loud,
familiar, and irritating. Louis Gaston, seated
just within the library door, heard every word
—as indeed he must have been deaf not to do—
and Margaret fancied she could detect an expression of angry superciliousness in the very
attitude of the well-set shoulders and the in-
clination of the close-cropped head.

The minutes came and went, until they
mounted up to hours, and still Major King
sat and talked and laughed and told jokes with
a ghastly hilarity, which his companion found
it frightfully hard to respond to. Nine o'clock
struck—ten, eleven, and still he did not go! It
could not be that he was enjoying himself, for
the poor girl felt that he was secretly as uncomfortable as herself, and, besides, he could

never have had a less entertaining companion.
She forced herself to attend, while he was giving an account of a play he had seen the night
before, which must have been lame and impo-
tent enough in the first instance, but which
in the rehash was intolerable.   She even
tried to laugh when he came to the amusing
parts, which he always indicated by laughing
loudly himself.   But it was torture to her.

All things have an end, however, an indis-
putable proposition with which Margaret had
buoyed herself up repeatedly during this trying
visit, and at last Major King rose to go.   He
was not going to be browbeaten into a hasty
retreat, however.   Not he!   He would take
his time about it, and by way of a parting assertion of ease, he took up a handsome book
from the table, and after reading the title
aloud, with a jocular air and a somewhat de-
fective pronunciation, he tossed it down so
carelessly that the beautiful *edition de luxe* fell
to the floor, with its delicate leaves crushed
open beneath its heavy cover.   He made no

effort to recover it, until he saw Margaret stooping to do so, when he hastily picked it up, and flung rather than placed it on the table. When Margaret had shaken hands with him, and said good-night, with no tinge of abatement of the courtesy which had characterized her conduct throughout, she looked toward the library and saw that Mr. Gaston had risen and turned toward them, bowing to Major King with exactly the same motion and expression as that with which he had acknowledged their introduction. There was one difference, however. The little frigid bow was given in perfect silence, and not one word of farewell was spoken. Major King responded by a short, defiant nod, and a flashing glance which might have surprised the other, had he allowed his gaze to rest upon the visitor's face long enough to perceive it.

There was a necessary delay in the hall over the rubbers and overcoat, which it seemed to Margaret that he put on with elaborate slowness, and then, at last, the front door closed behind Major King with a loud, contemptuous bang.

The ordeal was over, but it left poor Margaret with a heavy heart; she felt disgusted with everything and everybody.

"There's not a pin to choose between them," she was saying to herself, "only Mr. Gaston was the host, and Mr. Gaston is the more enlightened man, and therefore more bound to know better."

She was too angry to look at Louis, and was leaving the room with a quiet "good-night," when the young man arrested her by saying, in a tone of undisguised indignation:

"Twenty minutes past eleven o'clock; and a first visit too! This is intolerable!"

Margaret looked straight into his eyes, with a steady glance of scorn, that she made no effort to disguise.

"I dare say Major King was unaware of the lateness of the hour," she said, in a cool, high tone. "Good-night, Mr. Gaston."

And she walked quietly out of the room, and

mounted the stairs to her own apartment, angrier than she had been yet.

She closed the door behind her, turned the gas on full, and stretched herself out at her whole length on the lounge, clasping her hands under her head. Her thoughts were too confused to be formulated, but the one that predominated over all the rest was that she could never like Louis Gaston again. She had the feeling that would have made her wish to fight him had she been a man.

Major King's conduct had been in the highest degree reprehensible, but he had been led on to it by the slights the other offered him. And then, too, she had a keen perception of what Major King's opportunities had probably been. He belonged to the class of impoverished Southerners who had lost everything by the war, and had probably spent most of the years of his manhood in a small village, living in a style that formed a strong contrast to the affluence of his youth. His bearing, during this trying evening, she attributed much to ignorance and much to the stinging sense of failure and defeat, which the war had left on so many Southern men. Added to all this, there must have been a keen indignation at the unjustness and insolence with which he was treated by a man from whom he had a right to expect common civility at least.

But with Louis Gaston it was different. He could not plead the excuse of isolation and ignorance. He was a cultivated man of the world, who had all the advantages of education, travel, and wealth; and, more than all, his offence was heinous, in a Southern mind, because it had been committed against the stranger within the gates.

"Nothing can ever wipe it out," she muttered to herself; "the longer one thinks of it the worse it grows. There are half-a-dozen palliations for Major King, but for Mr. Gaston there is not one. I am certain that Major King, in spite of it all, would have been incapable of treating his worst enemy so. What a mortifying, humiliating experience!"

And, with a gesture of disgust, Miss Trevennon rose and walked to the dressing-table,
beginning slowly to unfasten her little orna-
ments, in preparation for the night's rest,
which, in her perturbed state of mind, was
very long in coming to her.

Louis Gaston, meanwhile, left to his own
reflections, grew conscious of the fact that he
was feeling very uncomfortable. The sensation was not by any means a new one. He had
harbored it, uninterruptedly, for the past three
hours, but it had undergone a change in kind
and degree. He was relieved from the intolerable infliction of Major King's presence, but
unrest in another form had entered his breast;
and though its nature was less tangible and aggressive, it somehow seemed to strike deeper.

He could not be blind to the fact that he
had offended Margaret, whose conduct during
the evening had really puzzled him as much
as his had puzzled her. How could she bear
to be pleasant and civil to a man like that? It
made him angry to think of the fellow's daring

even to speak to her, and he assured himself that he had been perfectly right to pursue a course which would free her from such an obnoxious intrusion in future. And yet, under it all, there was a glimmering, disturbing little consciousness that he had somehow been in the wrong. It was the first time in his life that he had had occasion to distrust his social methods, and he would not quite own to such a state of mind now. There was, moreover, another feeling at work within his breast, which caused him to determine that he would make some concessions, if necessary, to reinstate himself in this young lady's regard. It was a thing which he knew he had heretofore enjoyed, and he felt a strong reluctance to giving it up.

Neither were Louis Gaston's slumbers as serene and tranquil as usual that night. He made some effort to return to his work, but he found it impossible to fix his attention on it, and so retired to bed to wait for the sleep that was so strangely long in coming.

CHAPTER VII.

WHEN Miss Trevennon appeared at breakfast, the morning after Major King's visit, Mr. Gaston greeted her with more than his usual cordiality, and for the first time addressed her as "Miss Margaret."

The young lady replied to his morning salutation with a composed civility, and gave no sign of having observed the distinguished familiarity with which she was treated. She was quite her usual self during the meal, but she said little to Louis Gaston, and he observed that she did not voluntarily look at him. By the time that breakfast was ended she had managed, without awakening the least suspicion on the part of the others, to convey to Louis Gaston the conviction that she was set like steel against him.

It was at the same time depressing and inspiring to the young man to perceive this. He was sorry to have this charming girl angry with him, and yet he could well imagine how pleasant a reconciliation with her would be. He was certainly not a coxcomb, but he was accustomed to good-humored handling by women, and he had no misgivings as to his ability to adjust the present little difficulty to his entire satisfaction. Meantime, there she sat opposite, looking very charming, with her air of dainty reserve. The impertinent little ignoramus, to pretend to set *him* right! He smiled to himself at the absurdity of the thought. The situation seemed to him extremely piquant.

He had already settled upon the remark with which he would open the conversation, when he should presently follow her into the bow-window as usual, and he was therefore a little disconcerted when Miss Trevennon passed out of the dining-room by the door that opened into the hall, and mounted the stairs to her own room, whence she did not emerge until Louis, after long waiting, had gone off down town.

Later in the day, when Margaret found herself alone with Mrs. Gaston, she had some thought of informing the latter of last night's occurrences, but upon reflection this appeared so difficult that she gave it up. It was doubtful if any good purpose could be served thereby, and besides it would be very hard to describe her own feelings with sufficient reserve to avoid the rudeness of speaking unwarrantably to Mrs. Gaston of the brother-in-law who was such a favorite with her. Apart from all this, though there had been no opportunity for the positive manifestation of the feeling, it was borne in upon her that Mrs. Gaston herself would be found ranged on Louis' side. So she said nothing about the matter and listened to Cousin Eugenia's plans for the day just as usual.

There was another dinner on hand for this evening, and Mrs. Gaston expressed her intention of going out to recuperate her energies by a drive before luncheon, and Margaret presently left her, agreeing to join her, ready for

the expedition, at twelve.   In the hall she met
a servant with some letters, one of which
proved to be from her mother.   This letter,
filled with all manner of little, familiar domestic details, was read and re-read by Margaret with a degree of feeling quite inconsistent
with the nature of its contents.   The quiet
home-pictures presented such a contrast to
the annoyances recently encountered, that for
a while she heartily wished herself back at
Bassett.

There was but one item of especial importance in the letter, and that was the announcement of the sudden return from Europe of Mrs.
Trevennon's nephew, Alan Decourcy, an indi-
vidual who had long reigned in Margaret's
mind and memory as a veritable Prince Charming, who possessed to the letter every endow-
ment of nature and advantage of fortune which
the most exacting of maidens could have asked.
Margaret had not seen him since he had come
to man's estate, but, as a boy, he had spent
much of each year at a country home near Bas-

sett, owned by his mother, and she had always
looked upon him as the most fortunate and
gifted of beings. He was an only son, and his
sister, who was some years older than himself,
was now married and living in Baltimore. To
this sister Margaret had pledged herself for a
visit before returning to the South. How
pleasant it would be to meet Alan there! His
mother was now dead, and after finishing his
course at a Northern university he had gone
abroad for a year's travel, but it was only at
the end of four years that he had now returned.
She wondered if he would prove to be as handsome and charming as memory painted him!
His occasional letters had been very delightful,
and led her to believe that all the bright
promises of his youth had been fulfilled. And
now he had actually returned, and she was to
see him! Mrs. Trevennon wrote that she had
already sent him her daughter's address in
Washington, saying that he must run over
from Baltimore and see her. She added that
her nephew had said that he would probably

linger a while in New York before joining his sister, and so his movements were rather indefinite.

The feelings which this announcement of Alan Decourcy's return awakened were contradictory. Margaret was naturally very anxious to see this charming cousin, but she did not want him to come to see her in this house; she hoped she might never have another visitor here. Alan Decourcy was sure to be all that was elegant and charming, but since one person who had come to this house to see her had been treated with such discourtesy she wished for no more visitors. Already she had begun to lay plans for the termination of her visit, and she now resolved to speak to Cousin Eugenia, on the subject of going to Baltimore, as soon as the opportunity should offer.

"I wish I had Alan's New York address," she said to herself; "I'd write and tell him I would go to Baltimore, and so prevent his coming here. What *would* papa and mamma think if they knew I was staying at a house where I could not ask my cousin to call upon me, because I had no assurance that my visitors would not be treated rudely? They would not believe it. They simply could not understand it. My dear old father! He would take my letter to the light and read it over with his spectacles on, to see if there was not some mistake in his understanding of it. Once convinced, however, I know well enough what his course would be. He would write me to come away at once." And Margaret rose to prepare for her drive with eyes that had grown moist at these recollections of her far-off home.

By the time that Cousin Eugenia sent to summon her, however, Miss Trevennon had recovered her composure, and when, a little later, seated by her cousin's side, she was bowling swiftly over the smooth, hard pavements, the exhilaration of the exercise had roused her spirits to such buoyancy that small annoyances, past and future, seemed trivial enough to be ignored.

CHAPTER VIII.

HAVING assisted, humbly and admiringly, at Mrs. Gaston's elaborate dinner-toilet that evening, Margaret followed the gracefully cloaked and hooded figure down the stairs and out to the door-steps, when she said a gay good-by to her cousin and General Gaston, and turned and entered the house. She had been informed that Louis Gaston also had an engagement, and so she had the not unwelcome prospect of a quiet evening to herself. There were some things that she wanted leisure to think out, calmly and deliberately, and as the drawing-room looked very warm and inviting she turned toward it, and had sunk into her favorite chair before the fire, when she perceived, for the first time, that the library doors were thrown open and that Louis Gaston was sitting there at work. The sight was an irritating one. His very attitude and the set of his firm, strong shoulders, recalled vividly her discomfiture of the previous evening, and roused all the quick indignation she had felt then. She was about to withdraw at once, in the hope that he might not have perceived her entrance, when he turned suddenly, and, seeing her, rose and came forward, his face wearing its pleasantest smile, and his manner at its easiest and friendliest.

"Well, Cousin Margaret," he said, "and so they've left you behind! But I can assure you, you needn't regret it. The party is an old-fogy affair, which will be long and tedious. There's some glory to be got out of it, I dare say, but I'll wager there isn't much pleasure."

Margaret heard him deliver himself of these affable observations with intense indignation. "Cousin Margaret" indeed! Did he presume to suppose for an instant, that he could atone for the indignity he had offered her, and the positive pain he had caused her, by a few careless words of flattery and a caressing tone of voice?

"I shouldn't have cared to go with them in the least," she answered coldly. "I am used to quiet. Cousin Eugenia said you had an engagement."

"So I have; but that can be postponed, as also, I suppose, may be your meditations," answered Louis, feeling a keener zest in the accomplishment of this reconciliation with Margaret since he saw it was likely to cost him some pains. "Suppose now you and I run off to the theatre. There's a pretty little play on the boards, and we'll take our chances for a seat."

"Thank you, I don't care to go out this evening," responded Margaret, in the same voice.

There was a moment's silence, which might have lasted longer, but for some symptoms of flight on the part of Miss Trevennon, which the young man saw and determined to thwart.

"I am afraid," he began, speaking with some hesitation, "that I was so unfortunate as to offend you in some way last night, when your edifying visitor was here——"

"Please don't refer to that episode, unless you mean to apologize for what you did," Margaret interrupted him, with an inflection of controlled indignation. "Your laughing at him now does not mend matters."

The young man's whole expression changed. This was really a little too much.

"Apologize!" he said quickly, a dark frown gathering. "You are under some remarkable delusion, Miss Trevennon, if you think I acknowledge it to be a case for an apology. It was a most presumptuous intrusion, and as such I was compelled to resent it, on your account as well as my own."

"Don't let me be considered in the matter, I beg," said Margaret, with a little touch of scorn. "I wish no such deed as that to be done in my name."

"May I ask," said Gaston, in a keen, distinct voice, "whether your championship of this gentleman is due to an admiration and endorsement of his manner and conduct, or to the more comprehensive fact of his being a South-

erner ? You Southerners are very clannish, I've
been told."

Margaret had always held herself to be
superior to sectional prejudices, but there was
something in his manner, as he said this, that
infuriated her.

"We Southerners," she answered, feeling a
thrill of pride in identifying herself with the
race that, by his looks and tones, he was so
scornfully contemning, "are not only a clannish people, but also a courteous one, and the
very last and least of our number is incapable
of forgetting the sacred law of hospitality to a
guest."

Undoubtedly Miss Trevennon had forgotten
herself, but it was only for a moment. She
had said more than she meant to say, and she
checked herself with an effort, and added
hastily :

"I much prefer not to pursue this subject,
Mr. Gaston. We will drop it just here, if you
please."

The fact that Mr. Gaston bowed calmly, and

quietly returned to his work, by no means proved that he was in reality either calm or quiet. It was only by a great effort of self-control that he forced himself to be silent, for both the words and tones that this young lady had used were stingingly provoking. But what affected him most was the stunning presumptuousness of the whole thing. That this ignorant Southern girl, who had passed most of her life in a little insulated village, should venture to set him right on a point which affected his bearing as a man of the world, was infuriating. He mentally assured himself that his conduct toward the fellow, King, had been exactly what it should have been, and, moreover, he determined to take occasion to show Miss Trevennon that he neither regretted nor desired to apologize for it. He felt eager for an opportunity to do this, and all his accustomed prejudices and habits of mind grew deeper and stronger.

For a few moments longer they kept their places in perfect silence, Margaret in her seat before the fire and Gaston at the writing-table, when suddenly the door-bell rang. Neither moved nor spoke, and a few minutes later Thomas announced a gentleman to see Miss Trevennon.

"Alan Decourcy!" exclaimed Margaret, springing to her feet, in excited surprise, as the gentleman approached. "Why, Alan, this is unexpected!"

Mr. Decourcy came nearer, and taking both her hands in his, pressed them cordially.

"It would be ungrateful of me not to recognize my cousin Margaret, in this tall young lady," he said, looking at her with obvious admiration in his calm, gray eyes, "and yet it is only by an effort that I can do so."

At this instant Margaret remembered Louis, whom, in the confusion of this meeting, she had quite forgotten. She turned toward him, naming the two men to each other, and to her consternation she saw that he had risen, and was standing erect, with exactly the same repellant expression and attitude which he had assumed in greeting Major King the evening before. With the same frigid manner he acknowledged the present introduction, and after that little icy bow, he seated himself at his writing and turned his back, as before.

Mr. Decourcy, meantime, had taken a chair, from which Mr. Gaston's attitude was perfectly evident to him, but he showed quite as little concern thereat as Major King had done. And yet what a different thing was this form of self-possession! Mr. Decourcy's low-toned sentences were uttered with a polished accent that told, as plainly as all the words in the dictionary could have done, that he was a man of finished good-breeding. He treated Margaret with an affectionate deference that she could not fail to find extremely pleasing; inquired for Mr. and Mrs. Trevennon, and said he was determined to go down to see the old home and friends before the winter was over; told Margaret he was glad she had verified his predictions by growing tall and straight; asked if they still called her Daisy at home, and whether it would be accounted presumptuous for him to do so; said very little indeed of himself and his travels, and at the end of about fifteen minutes rose to take leave.

Margaret quietly replied to all his questions, and when he held out his hand to say good-by, she made no motion to detain him, by word or sign.

"I am going back to Baltimore in a day or two," he said, "and shall hardly see you again, but I hope you will allow me to arrange for a visit from you to my sister, to take place very soon. When she writes to you on the subject, as she will do at once, do let her find you willing to co-operate with her."

While Margaret was uttering a hearty assent to this plan, Louis Gaston, who had, of course, heard all that had passed, was rapidly casting about in his mind as to how he should rescue himself from an odious position. There was now no more time to deliberate. He must act; and accordingly he came forward, with a return to his usual manner, which

Margaret had once thought so good, and said frankly :

"I happened to have an important bit of work on hand, Mr. Decourcy, which it was necessary for me to finish in haste. I have been obliged, therefore, to forego the pleasure of making your acquaintance, but I hope you will give me your address that I may call upon you."

"Thank you, I am at the Arlington for a day or two," responded Decourcy, with his polished politeness of tone and manner, in which Margaret felt such a pride at the moment.

"It is quite early," Louis went on, "and my brother and sister have deserted Miss Trevennon for a dinner. Will you not remain and spend the evening with her?"

Alan Decourcy possessed to perfection the manner which George Eliot describes as "that controlled self-consciousness which is the expensive substitute for simplicity," and it was apparently with the most perfect naturalness that he pleaded another engagement and took leave, with compliments and regards to General and Mrs. Gaston. The price this young man had paid for this manner was some years of studious observance of what he considered the best models at home and abroad, and his efforts had been eminently successful. It imposed upon Margaret completely, and charming though she saw her cousin to be, she would have said that his manners were as unstudied as a child's.

Louis Gaston, on his part, considered the matter more understandingly. He recognized in this cousin of Miss Trevennon a polished man of the world. The type was familiar enough to him, but he knew that this was an exquisite specimen of it, and the very fineness of Mr. Decourcy's breeding made his own recent bearing seem more monstrously at fault. He felt very anxious to set himself right with Miss Trevennon at once, but almost before he had time to consider the means of doing this she had said good-night and gone up stairs.

He stood where she had left him, abstracted and ill at ease. What a power this girl had of making him feel uncomfortable; for it was not Decourcy's censure and disapprobation that he deprecated half so much as Margaret's. Again there came into his breast that new, strange feeling of self-distrust. He shook it off with a sigh, tired of self-communing and reflection, and anxious to act. He felt his present position unendurable.

Accordingly, he rang for Thomas and sent him to ask Miss Trevennon if he could speak to her for a few minutes. Thomas carried the message, and presently returned to say that Miss Trevennon would come down.

When she entered the room, soon after, she looked so stately, and met his eyes with such a cold glance, that a less determined man might have faltered. He was very much in earnest, however, and so he said at once:

"I ventured to trouble you to return, Miss Trevennon, in order that I might apologize to you for what I acknowledge to have been an act of rudeness. I am exceedingly sorry for it, and I ask your pardon."

"You have it, of course, Mr. Gaston. An offence acknowledged and regretted is necessarily forgiven. I want you to tell me explicitly, however, what act you refer to."

"I feel myself to have acted unwarrantably, indeed rudely, in my manner of receiving your cousin. I was angry at the time, and I forgot myself. I have done what little I could to atone for it to Mr. Decourcy, but I felt that I owed you an apology, because in acting thus toward a guest of yours I was guilty of a rudeness to you."

Margaret was silent; but how she burned to speak!

"Am I forgiven?" said Gaston, after a little pause, for the first time smiling a little, and speaking in the clear, sweet tones that she had lately thought the pleasantest in the world. If she thought so still, she denied it to her own heart.

"I need hardly say, Mr. Gaston," she

answered, forcing back a sigh, "that as far as I am concerned, you have quite atoned for your treatment of my cousin."

"Then am I reinstated in your favor, great Queen Margaret, and will you give me your royal hand upon it?"

He extended his hand, but Margaret quickly clasped hers with its fellow, and dropped them in front of her, while she slowly shook her head. There was none of the bright *naïveté* so natural to her, in this action; she looked thoughtful and very grave.

The young man felt his pulses quicken; he resolved that she should make friends with him, cost what it might. It had become of the very first importance to him that he should be reinstated in that place in her regard which he knew that he had once held, and which he now felt to be so priceless a treasure.

"I am still unforgiven, I see," he said; "but you will at least tell me what is my offence that I may seek to expiate it."

Margaret raised her candid eyes to his and

looked at him a moment with a strange expression; doubt, disappointment and glimmering hope were mingled in it.

"Shall I be frank with you?" she said, speaking from a sudden impulse. "I should like to, if I dared."

"I shall be distressed if you are not," he said, almost eagerly. "I beg you to say freely what you have in your mind."

She did not speak at once, but sank into a chair, with a long-drawn respiration that might mean either sadness or relief. When Gaston had brought another chair and placed it close beside her and seated himself, she looked up and met his gaze. In the eyes of both there was the eagerness of youth—in the girl's a hesitating wistfulness, in the man's a subdued fire, somewhat strange to them. He was conscious of being deeply stirred, and if he had spoken first his words would probably have betrayed this, but it was Margaret who broke the silence, in tones that were calm and steady, and a little sad.

"Mr. Gaston," she said, turning her eyes away from his face and looking into the fire, "it wouldn't be worth while, I think, for me to pretend to feel the same toward you, after what has happened; it would be only pretence. Twenty-four hours ago I should have said you were the young man of all my acquaintance. whom I felt to be the truest gentleman. I would not say this to your face now, except that it is quite passed."

"I am glad that you have said it—most glad that it was ever so," he said, with a hurried ardor; "but it is a great height to fall from. And have I indeed fallen?"

"Yes," replied Margaret, not smiling at all, but speaking very gravely. "You began to fall the moment Major King came into this room last night, and you have been falling ever since, as I have gone over it all in my mind. You reached the bottom when my cousin came in this evening, and the shock was so great that it caused a slight rebound; but I don't suppose that signifies much."

If the girl's eyes had not been fixed upon the fire she would probably have checked her speech at the sight of the expression which settled upon her companion's face the moment Major King's name was mentioned. But she did not see it, and was therefore unprepared for the hard, cold tone in which his next words were uttered.

"I have felt and acknowledged my fault, where your cousin was concerned," he said. "Mr. Decourcy is a gentleman, and nothing but the fact of my being preoccupied with the resentment I felt at certain words of yours at the time, would have caused me to act toward him as I did. This explains, but does not justify my conduct, which I have acknowledged to be unjustifiable. But in the other case, Miss Trevennon, I must maintain that I acted rightly."

"If that is your feeling about it," Margaret said, "I think this conversation had better end here."

"Why, Miss Trevennon?" he asked, a

little defiantly. "I see no reason why it should."

"Because its object, as I suppose, has been to bring about an understanding between us; and since you have defined your sentiments, it is clear to me that we could no more come to understand each other than if you spoke Sanscrit and I spoke French."

"I believe you are mistaken," he said. "I have a feeling that our positions are not so widely different as they may appear to be. Don't refuse to listen to me, Miss Trevennon; that would be unjust, and you are not an unjust woman."

It was a wonderful proof of the hold she had laid upon him that he took such trouble to exonerate himself in her eyes, and he felt it so himself, but he no longer denied the fact that Miss Trevennon's good opinion was a matter of vast importance to him. The little impulses of anger which her severe words now and then called forth, were always short lived. One glance at the lovely face and figure near

him was generally enough to banish them,
and now, as he treated himself to a long look
at the fair countenance, with its sweet down-
cast eyes and slightly saddened mouth, the im-
possibility of quarrelling with this exquisite
creature presented itself so strongly, that he
grew suddenly so friendly and at ease, that he
was able to assume a tone that was pleasant,
and almost gay, as he said :

"Now, Miss Trevennon, honor bright! You
know perfectly well that you don't like that
man one bit better than I do."

"I don't like him at all. I yield that point
at once, but I fail to see how that affects the
matter. Children and savages regulate their
manners according to their tastes and fancies,
but I had always supposed that well-bred men
and women had a habit of good-breeding that
outside objects could not affect."

"A gentleman's house is his castle, Miss
Trevennon," said Gaston, with a return to his
former tone and manner; "and it is one of the
plainest and most sacred of his duties to see

that the ladies of his household are protected from all improper contact. In my brother's absence I stood in the position of the gentleman of the house, and I did right to adopt a line of conduct which would save you from a like intrusion in future. I owed it to you to do so."

"I beg your pardon," said Margaret, waving her hand with a pretty little motion of scornful rejection. " You allowed your consideration for me to constrain you too far. I have led a free, unrestricted life, and am accustomed to contact with those who come and go. No man has a finer feeling as to what is fitting for the ladies of his family than my father, but though I should live to reach old age, I shall never see him pay so great a price for my immunity from doubtful association as an act of rudeness to any one whomsoever."

" I'll tell you what it is, Miss Trevennon," said Gaston, speaking rather warmly, " if you lived in Washington, you would see things differently. There's no end to the pushing impertinence of the people who hang about a city—this one especially, and a gentleman does not like to have his friends in danger of meeting these obnoxious creatures at his house. It looks very queer, and people think so, too."

"Is a gentleman's position, then, so easily impeached? Now I should have thought that, with your name and prestige, you might weather a good many queer appearances. An annoyance of this sort would not be likely to happen often. That it is an annoyance, I do not deny; but I think there must be a better way of preventing such things than the one you adopted. And oh, Mr. Gaston, while we are on this subject, I wonder how you can ignore one point, the agony that you caused me!"

"That *I* caused you, Miss Trevennon? It is hard, indeed, to lay at my door the discomfiture you endured last evening."

"I think it was the most wretched evening I ever passed," said Margaret, "and it was only your conduct that made it so."

"My conduct? Now you *are* unjust!"

"Not at all," said Margaret. "I am not so wholly uninured to the necessity of sometimes bearing annoyances, as to be made miserable by having to talk for several hours with a man I do not like. You will never believe it, of course, but I do not think Major King is a man who lacks good feeling, the essence and soul of politeness. He belongs to a type that I know very well. He is an ignorant man and a very self-opinionated one, and he has been so long in need of association with his superiors that he has begun to think that he has none. He does not know the world, and is therefore unaware of the fact, that a man who holds the position of a gentleman may be guilty of many lapses without losing that position. I spoke just now of its being rather a light tenure, but, in some ways, it is very strong, it seems. I have said I do not like Major King, but I believe it is a mistake to call him vulgar. He is foolish and conceited, because he has had very slender opportunities to learn better. But oh, Mr. Gaston, how different with you! It is impossible not to draw the contrast. You know the world. You have studied and travelled. You are clever, cultivated and accomplished, and to what end? It has all resulted in an act which yesterday I would have wagered my right hand you were incapable of."

She spoke with real feeling in her voice, and Gaston caught this inflection, and the sound of it quickened his blood. His ideas and emotions were strangely confused. He felt that he ought to be angry and resentful, but he was conscious only of being contrite.

"I have said too much. I have spoken far too freely," said Margaret, breaking in upon his reflections. "I meant to be quite silent, but when you urged me to speak I forgot myself. I am sorry."

"Don't be," the young man answered gently; " the fact that these are your opinions entitles them at least to my respect. But there is one thing I must mention before we drop this subject. I cannot be satisfied to allow you to retain the idea that I was accountable for the discomfiture you endured yesterday evening. You must know that I would joyfully shield you from all vexations and annoyances."

"No," said Margaret gently, shaking her head; "it was you, and not Major King, who made those hours so wretched to me. You made no effort to conceal the fact that you were outraged and indignant, and what could be clearer than that I had been the means of bringing this deeply resented annoyance upon you? If you had thought of me, you must have seen that."

"I thought of you continually. It was chiefly upon your account that I resented the intrusion. It matters little to a man whom he happens to rub against, but it pains me deeply that a lady—that *you* should not be screened from such intercourse."

In spite of herself, Margaret was touched by this. A hundred times, since she had known him, she had seen Louis Gaston give evidence of an exquisite feeling of deference to women, and she could readily believe that he had been influenced on this occasion partly by consideration for herself; and while she resented the means used she did justice to the motive.

"It is much better that we have talked of this," she said presently. "I do thank you for having that feeling about me. You could not know it was not needed. I will try to forget it all."

" But you will not succeed," he said; "your tone convinces me of that. I wish we understood each other better, Miss Trevennon, and I do not yet give up the hope that in time we may."

He drew out his watch and looked at it, saying in tones that showed him to be in a serious mood:

"I have an appointment to see a man on business, and I must go and keep it. I shall probably be late coming in, and shall hardly see you again, so I'll say good-night."

As he spoke, he turned and went into the

hall, and a moment later Margaret heard the front door close behind him.

As she slowly mounted the stairs to her room, she remembered that he had not asked her again to shake hands with him, in token of a re-establishment of the old relationship between them, and, on the whole, she did not regret it. It was as well that he should know that he was not restored to his former place in her regard. Her faith in him had been terribly shaken, and it seemed impossible he could ever be to her again the man she had once thought him.

CHAPTER IX.

WHEN Mrs. Gaston and Miss Trevennon were driving along the avenue next morning, the former said abruptly, "Why didn't you tell me of your cousin's visit?"

"Oh, I didn't see you when you came in, you know," answered Margaret evasively. "Who told you?"

"Louis: and I gathered from certain indications that there had been something unpleasant in this meeting. I didn't ask him to explain it to me, and I don't ask you. I hate explanations. I have always foreseen that a certain amount of clashing was inevitable between you and Louis. You are both very well in your ways, but your ways are very different and not very reconcilable. I am very sorry anything of the sort happened; but I don't let it prey upon my mind, and I hope you will not either."

"Oh no," said Margaret; "it was nothing very important. Mr. Gaston was rude to Alan when he first came in, but he atoned for it as far as he could afterward."

At this moment a handsome drag containing two gentlemen and a liveried servant was seen approaching, and, as it came up to them, one of the gentlemen recognized Margaret with a bow and a smile.

"There's Alan now!" said Margaret. "I wonder who the gentleman is, who is driving."

"It's young Lord Waring," said Mrs. Gaston, with animation. "He is attached to the British Legation—the minister's nephew, I believe. And so that was Alan Decourcy! What a charming young man! I wonder how Louis could be rude to a man like that."

It was Margaret's usual habit to pass over such remarks as this from Cousin Eugenia, as she was convinced of the fruitlessness of argument in her case; but this speech touched her on such a sore point that she could not help saying, in rather keen tones :

"A man who could be rude to any one whomsoever, must be somewhat difficult to count upon, I should think. He must be often puzzled to decide whom to treat civilly and whom to snub."

"Oh, there you go, with your high-flown Southern notions," retorted Mrs. Gaston, with imperturbable good-humor. "You're your father's own child! But we must have this elegant young man to dinner. Do you happen to know if he is engaged for this evening?"

"No," said Margaret, "I didn't hear him say."

"He will probably call during the day."

"No, he will not," said Margaret, decidedly. "He told me he should not see me again before going to Baltimore. But he is to make arrangements for me to go over for a little visit soon, and I shall see him then."

"Nonsense! He's to come and see you at my house, and he's to make friends with us all. Louis has been in the wrong, and he shall be made to see it. Leave that to me. I shall write

young Decourcy a note as soon as I get home ;
and you shall write too, and endorse my invitation."

Margaret felt very anxious that her cousin
should come and dine at the Gastons', but she
seriously doubted his willingness to do so.
Despite his perfect courtesy, there had been
something in his manner toward Louis Gaston
that made it clear that he did not desire to improve the latter's acquaintance, and she wanted
him to see that in the interview he had had
with Gaston he had seen Louis at his worst, and
to realize that he had a better side. And, on
the other hand, she wanted the Gastons to see
Alan Decourcy as a specimen of a Southern
gentleman, who not only possessed, by inheritance, all the instincts and traditions that she
clung to and respected, but who, in addition
to these, had had sufficient contact with the
world to get rid of that colossal belief in himself and his own methods and manners, as the
only commendable ones, which she felt to be
one of the chief failings of her countrymen.

She had been too long accustomed to the arrogant assumption that a Southern man had better take the wrong way in any issue than learn the right way from a Yankee, not to rejoice in the prospect of presenting to her friends a young Southerner who was really enlightened, and who, if he loved his own land best, did so because he had compared it with others, and not because he was ignorant of everything beyond it.

But when Mrs. Gaston had despatched her note, inviting Mr. Decourcy to dine with them that evening at six, and there came a response regretting that a previous engagement for dinner prevented his accepting her invitation, Mrs. Gaston was quite provoked about it, and when they were at dinner she confided her disappointment to her husband and his brother.

"I called on him at the Arlington, this morning," said Louis, "but he was out."

"Yes, we met him," said Mrs. Gaston. "He was driving with Lord Waring."

Margaret felt a little throb of gratification, as her cousin made this announcement, of which she was deeply ashamed the next instant. "I am getting the most horrid ideas into my head," she said to herself; "what a little snob I should have felt myself two months ago, to be filled with vulgar elation at the thought of Alan Decourcy being seen driving with a lord! It's perfectly humiliating!" But all the same, the satisfaction remained.

"I wonder where he is going to dine," Mrs. Gaston went on, presently. "He will call, of course, in acknowledgment of my invitation, and when he does, Margaret, you must ask him."

The next morning he did call, and Mrs. Gaston and Margaret were at home to receive him. Margaret asked him, in the course of their talk, where he had dined the day before, and convicted herself a second time of snobbishness by the pleasure she felt in hearing him answer:

"At the British Legation. The minister

happens to be an old acquaintance, and Waring and I were great chums at one time. By-
the-way, he was, for some reason, rather struck
with you, Daisy. He was with me when I
met you driving yesterday, you remember. I
told him you were a pet cousin of mine, and it
may have been on that account that he asked
me to bring him to call upon you."

"I hope you will do so," Mrs. Gaston said.
"We should be glad to see him."

There was no under-bred eagerness in her
tones as she said it, but Margaret suspected
that there might be a little in her heart, and
she was not sorry when Decourcy answered,
merely:

"Thank you; you're very kind," and then
changed the subject by saying:

"I picked up a little present for you, when
I was in Naples, Margaret. I unpacked it this
morning and will send it to you."

A few minutes after this he took leave,
having made on both ladies an extremely good
impression, which Mrs. Gaston owned to, in

voluble phrases, and which Margaret concealed under a very calm exterior.

A day or two later Alan called again, and brought with him Lord Waring, who proved to be a little dull. He was shy and constrained in manner and hampered by a certain gawkiness which Decourcy's exquisite ease of breeding made the more apparent. In spite of all this, however, there was something rather distinguished in the young foreigner, a sincerity and simplicity that stamped him as a man of worth, and a commanding self-security that was as far removed from self-sufficiency as possible.

It was arranged between Miss Trevennon and her cousin that they were to go to Baltimore in a few days, and it was not until he rose to take leave that he put into her hands a box, which he told her contained the little present he had spoken of.

As soon as the two gentlemen had gone, Margaret tore open the parcel with the eagerness of a girl to whom presents are somewhat rare, and discovered, in a beautiful little

mosaic box, an antique silver chatelaine of the
most rare and exquisite workmanship.   There
was a small watch, and other richly chased
pendents, and the whole thing was pretty
enough to delight any girl alive, even in the
absence of a just appreciation of its value.
Cousin Eugenia, however, being thoroughly
initiated in all such matters, was handling and
examining it with a depth of appreciation that
almost brought tears to her eyes.

"Why, Margaret, it is a superb present," she
exclaimed ; "a veritable antique, such as not
one woman in a thousand is lucky enough to
possess.   You *must* let me show it to Mrs.
Norman ; she is continually flaunting hers in
peoples' faces, and it doesn't compare with this.
I should say it is quite modern beside this.
Just look at these clasps.   The watch is not
so antique, but the chains and clasps are wonderful."

Margaret, as she looked on and listened, could
scarcely conceal the amusement she felt.   She
had often before this had reason to observe

the almost solemn emotion with which Cousin
Eugenia was wont to regard certain articles of
great luxuriousness or magnificence. She had
seen her stirred to the soul by a plush *portière*,
and almost tearful at the mere recollection of
a French costume. Appreciation was one
thing, but this was another. It transcended
mere appreciation, and seemed, in some way,
to be tinctured with the heroic.

"What an æsthete you would have made,
Cousin Eugenia, if only the proper influences
had been brought to bear!" said Margaret,
laughing. "I can fancy you speaking, in
awed and hushed accents, of a strange and
mysterious color, or a significant and subtle
bit of drapery. You consider yourself unemotional, but you have depths which may be
stirred. It takes a silver chatelaine of a rare
order to compass it, however, or something as
imposing. I have to thank you for enlight-
ening me as to the value of Alan's gift. If
I tell him you wept upon it, it may compensate
in some measure for my Philistinism."

"He must have taken great care in the selection of this present for you," Mrs. Gaston said. "He admires you very much, Margaret. I begin to wonder what it means."

Margaret laughed gayly.

"It means nothing whatever," she said; "for goodness' sake, don't get up any absurd notion about Alan Decourcy and me. It's a brand-new idea."

"To you it may be—not to him. He has a way of watching you that means something. A careful, scrutinizing interest in all you do is observable, and often it changes into those quiet signs of approbation, which mean so much in a man like that. I shall be prepared for a prompt surrender, so don't be afraid of startling me if you have anything to communicate from Baltimore. He told me the other day, that he had reached an eminently marriageable age, and was dreadfully afraid of passing beyond it. He also said that he much preferred to marry one of his own countrywomen; and I believe that is what brings him home."

Margaret gave an amused attention to her cousin's speculations, after which they fell to talking of the proposed visit to Baltimore, which Cousin Eugenia acquiesced in only on condition that it should be of but one week's duration, and that Margaret should return to Washington for Christmas. This she agreed to do, resolving, if she found it desirable, to arrange for another visit before returning to the South.

CHAPTER X.

MARGARET had been, from the first, eager to hear Decourcy's criticism of the Gastons, and when she found herself seated by her cousin's side, in the train on the way to Baltimore, with the prospect of an hour's *tête-à-tête* before her, she felt sure he would volunteer his impressions. She only hoped that he would remember that, in spite of all, she really liked them, and that he would refrain from speaking too resentfully on the subject. She was full of unuttered criticism herself, but a feeling of loyalty to the friends who had shown her so much kindness deterred her from introducing the topic. It soon appeared, however, that Mr. Decourcy had no intention of speaking of it at all. Of course they talked about the Gastons, but it was only in incidental allusions, and, after all, it was Margaret who invited his criticism by saying directly :

" What do you think of them, Alan ? "

" Oh, pretty well," he answered lightly.
" The General is a little heavy, but his wife
has vivacity enough to counterbalance him, and
I should say the brother is a fine fellow."

Margaret's eyes opened wide with astonishment. Forgetting all her good resolutions,
now that she and her cousin had so decidedly
shifted positions, she said excitedly :

" Why, Alan, I supposed you thought him
simply intolerable."

Her cousin, in his turn, looked surprised.

" You know him better than I," he said,
" and it may be that that is his real character ;
but I met him at the club the other night and
was rather struck with him. It may be all surface, however. He is a good-looking fellow—
and has very good manners.".

" Good manners ! Oh, Alan ! His conduct,
the first time you met him, was really terrible ;
it filled me with shame for him."

" Oh yes ; I remember that very well," said
Decourcy, quietly ; " but I rather fancied, from

certain signs, that that was mostly due to his being at odds with you, in some way. Yes," he went on, looking faintly amused at the reminiscence, "he evidently intended to annihilate me, but when he saw that he had better not think of it, I must say he gave up with a good grace, and since then he has done everything in his power to manifest an intention to be civil. In this condition of affairs, I find him a very likeable, intelligent fellow."

"And you bear him no grudge for the manner in which he treated you?"

"My dear Daisy! what's the use of bearing grudges? Life is much too short. And besides, a great many people are like that."

"What sort of people? Vulgar people and ignorant people, I suppose!"

"Well, not necessarily. I have often seen such conduct from people whom I could not, on the whole, call either ignorant or vulgar. It seems to be the instinct with some men to consider every stranger a blackguard, until he has proved himself not to be one."

"It is abominable," said Margaret; "perfectly barbarous! Such people have no right
to claim to be civilized."

"In point of fact, it is only a very small class,
my dear, who can justly lay claim to that estate.
I understand your feeling. How it carries me
back! I used to feel much as you do, before I
went out into the world."

"I should think a knowledge of the world
would make one more fastidious instead of less
so," said Margaret, sturdily.

"I think you are wrong in that. One learns
to take things as they come, and loses the
notion of having all things exactly to one's
taste."

"But surely such flagrant impoliteness as
Mr. Gaston's would be condemned anywhere,"
said Margaret. "You should have seen his
treatment of Major King."

She then proceeded to give a spirited account of that episode, to her cousin's manifest
interest and amusement.

"And how your hot Southern blood did

tingle!" he commented, as she ended her recital. "You felt as if a crime had been committed in your sight, which it was your sacred duty to avenge—did you not? I had such feelings once myself, and perhaps, in both our cases, they may be traced to the same cause. Constant observation of such a model as your father presents would put most of the world at a disadvantage. There is a fineness of grain in him that one meets with but rarely anywhere. With him the feeling is that every man must be regarded and treated as a gentleman, until he has proved himself not to be one. It is a better way. But I think, after all, Margaret, that absolute good-breeding is a thing we must look for in individuals, and not in classes. It certainly does not exist in any class with which I have been thrown, and I cannot quite see how it could, as long as our social system of standards and rewards remains what it is. Do you remember a clever squib in *Punch*, *àpropos* of all this?"

Margaret shook her head.

"I very rarely see *Punch*," she said.

" It represents a conversation on the deck of an ocean steamer, between a beautiful American girl, returning from Europe, and several Englishmen, who are grouped about her. One of these is saying : ' Now, Miss——, do tell us. You've travelled a great deal, and seen the world, where have you met with the most elegant, refined, and high-bred men and women ? ' ' Among your British aristocracy,' replies the young lady, frankly. Her response is greeted with a flutter of delight by the group, and their spokesman puts another question : ' Now tell us, on the other hand,' he says, ' where you have met with the greatest ill-breeding and vulgarity.' The answer comes as promptly as before : ' Among your British aristocracy.' That," proceeded Decourcy, after waiting for Margaret's ready tribute of appreciation, " according to my own small experience, states the case exactly, and, with certain limitations, the same thing is true of the aristocracy of every country. A low-born ignoramus could never be the finished snob that a man of some enlightenment may be; he wouldn't know how. But confess, Margaret,—hot little rebel as you are!—have you never encountered the elements of snobbishness among your own people?"

"Yes; but I always supposed it came from ignorance and was greatly due to the fact that, since the war, our people have had so little opportunity of seeing the world, and have become insulated and prejudiced in consequence."

"There is something in that; but it was always so, I fancy, more or less. We are by nature and habit a self-opinionated race, with certain honorable exceptions, of course. But this I will say—by way of a little private swagger between ourselves—that I think we are a courteous people, indeed the most courteous I have known, with more inherent good-feeling for others. That ought to comfort you."

"Yes," said Margaret, rather wistfully; "but there are so many other things. Our people are so indolent, it seems to me—at least since the war."

"You always make me laugh, Daisy, when you introduce that little phrase, ' since the war.' You seem to find in it a satisfactory excuse for all the delinquencies of your beloved people. But the South, my sweet cousin, has never been a Utopia, any more than other lands. Wheat and tares must grow together everywhere."

" I am glad you call them my beloved people," said Margaret, after a little silence. " At home they do not think me very patriotic."

"Whom do you mean by ' they ' ? "

" I was thinking of Charley Somers——"

" Oh, by-the-way, I meant to ask about that pretty young fellow," said Decourcy. "I used to make him very angry by telling him he ought to induce Bassett to take a newspaper, and suggesting that the name of the town should be changed to Cosmopolis. I am afraid Charley never loved me. I shudder still at the remembrance of the scowls he would cast upon me whenever I went near you. How is he?"

"Very well," said Margeret; "not changed at all."

"He hasn't followed my advice about the paper, then? How about his voice? It bid fair to be superb. I hope it has developed well."

"I don't think it has developed at all," said Margaret. "Certainly it has had no training worthy the name. It is a shame to see him throwing that magnificent gift away. I have thought of it so much, in hearing Mr. Gaston sing. He has no voice at all, compared to Charley's, but he has spent such patient labor on its cultivation that his method is exquisite, and his singing would charm any one. Isn't it a fine thing to think how he worked over it, while all the time he was studying hard at his profession too."

"So Gaston is lucky enough to have won your approbation, in one quarter, at least, though he does come under your ban in another," said Decourcy. " You are exacting, Margaret, and severe in your ideals : I foresee that I shall be afraid of you. It would be interesting to make the acquaintance of the lucky man who is destined to command your entire approval, and win your fair hand."

Margaret laughed brightly :

" Cousin Eugenia says I shall never marry," she answered ; " she says I expect as much as if I were an heiress, and a beauty, and an intellectual prodigy, all in one. But I tell her my comfort is that the sort of man I should care for invariably falls in love with his inferior."

At this point the train glided into the station, and the conversation between the cousins came to an end.

11

CHAPTER XI.

UNDER the stimulating pressure of recent experiences Margaret had taken up her music again, with great ardor and determination. Mr. Gaston had encouraged her to believe that she might yet make a good performer, and had managed to instil into her some of his own spirit of thinking it worth while to achieve the best attainable, even though great proficiency might be out of reach. There was so little time during the day when she could count upon remaining in undisturbed possession of the piano that, for some time before leaving Washington, she had been in the habit of rising earlier and practising for an hour before breakfast, and she was resolved that her visit to Baltimore should not interfere with this routine. Indeed, she would have felt its interruption to be a serious moral retrogression, and so, with Mrs. Guion's sanction, she kept up her morning labors, and when the family met at breakfast every day, she had already accomplished her allotted period of practising. Alan used to laugh at her about it, and tell her she was becoming Yankeeized. He was apt to be late for breakfast himself, and Mrs. Guion took a great deal of trouble in having things kept hot for him, and would arrange little delicacies for him, much as if he had been an invalid lady, as Margaret more than once remarked with a certain degree of impatience. It quite irritated her to see how his sister pampered and indulged him and how carelessly, and as a matter of course, he accepted it all.

The Guions had only recently come to Baltimore from the South. Their old home had been very near to Margaret's, and she had consequently seen much more of Mrs. Guion, of late years, than of Alan. The children, of whom there were three, ranging from two to seven years of age, were cherished acquaintances of Margaret's, and hailed her arrival with a hearty enthusiasm, that she responded to with much cordiality. Ethel, the eldest, had been taught by her mother, long ago, to call Miss Trevennon "Auntie Margaret," and Amy and Decourcy had, of course, adopted the title. They were charming children, rather delicate in health, and watched and guarded with such care by their anxious mother, that they had the air of frail exotics. Mr. Guion had died when Decourcy was a baby, and it was because Alan had decided to settle in Baltimore for the practise of his profession, the law, that Mrs. Guion had moved her little family there. She was enthusiastically attached to her only brother, and never wearied of discoursing upon his perfections and displaying the numberless useful and ornamental presents that he lavished upon her children and herself.

"Wasn't it good of Alan to insist upon our coming to Baltimore, that he might make his home with us?" said Mrs. Guion, talking to her young cousin, the day after the latter's arrival. "So many young men would have thought it a nuisance to be hampered by a woman and three children; but he insisted on our coming."

"I can hardly see how he could regard you in the light of a nuisance," said Margaret, smiling; "your chief object in life seems to be to humor his whims and caprices. He could certainly not secure such comfort as you administer to him, in any bachelor-quarters on earth."

This view of the case had never occurred to Mrs. Guion, and she rejected it almost indignantly, and argued long to convince her cousin that she was, in all respects, the favored one; but without much success.

It was by a mere accident that Margaret discovered, a day or two after her arrival, that Alan's sleeping-apartment, situated just above the front drawing-room, had been exchanged for one on the other side of the hall. In an instant it flashed upon her that her morning performance on the piano had been the cause of it. To be quite certain, however, she went to Mrs. Guion and asked her directly of it was not so.

"How did you find it out?" said Mrs. Guion; "you were not to know anything about it. The other room is quite as convenient for Alan. He says he likes it just as well, and he wouldn't for the world have you know that he moved on that account. But, you know, he never could bear noise. Even the children understand that they must be quiet when he is here."

"Is he an invalid, in any way?" asked Margaret.

"Oh, dear no! but he always had that objection to noise, and I think he is more set in his ways now than ever. I tell him he ought to marry."

"If he values his personal ease so much, it might be a mistake to imperil it by matrimony," said Margaret, with a touch of contempt in her voice not discernible to her unsuspecting cousin.

"Affluence and idleness have made him luxurious," said Margaret to herself, reflectively, when Mrs. Guion had left her alone. " I suppose those two things are apt to go together. And yet Cousin Eugenia says Mr. Gaston has always been well off, and certainly the veriest pauper could not work harder! And still——"

The sentence ended in a little sigh. There was no denying the fact that Louis Gaston's descent from the pedestal upon which she had mentally placed him, had been a great blow.

Miss Trevennon's time passed very agreeably in Baltimore. Mrs. Guion, as yet, had only a small circle of friends, but most of these called upon her cousin, and several invitations resulted from these visits. As to Alan, the number of invitations he received was quite amusing. He had been twice to the club, and had delivered only one or two of his various letters, and made only one or two visits, when the cards of invitation began to pour in. He happened to have a few desirable acquaintances in Baltimore, his appearance was distinguished, and he was known to be rich, and these three facts, taken together, sufficiently account for the degree of popularity of which he found himself possessed.

One thing that rather surprised Margaret was the readiness with which her cousin would throw aside other engagements in order to drive her out, or take her to the theatre, or contribute, in any way, to her enjoyment. He even stayed at home one whole rainy evening, when Mrs. Guion was engaged up-stairs with one of the children, who was unwell, in order, as he distinctly avowed, to have a long talk with her.

When Miss Trevennon and Mr. Decourcy found themselves alone in the drawing-room, the latter threw himself, at full length, upon a low lounge, drawn up before the fire, and, fixing his eyes enjoyingly on Margaret, as she sat opposite, he drew a long breath of restful satisfaction, saying :

"Now this is real enjoyment. You don't

know it, perhaps, but it is just what I have longed for. Amy has really done this room charmingly, and has contrived to get precisely the atmosphere I like in it. The confusion of sweet and pungent odors from those plants yonder is just faint enough to be agreeable ; and, far above all, my fair cousin, with her silken draperies and beautiful pose, puts a climax to my happiness. You have a talent for attitude, my Marguerite—do you know it? You always place yourself to advantage. I don't know whether it is nature or art, but it is equally admirable, in either case."

Margaret, who sat in a deep chair with her arms laid along its padded sides, and her hands lightly clasping the rounded ends, her long silk gown falling away to the left, while her figure was slightly turned toward her cousin at her right, fixed her eyes upon the points of her little slippers, crossed before her, and remained profoundly still.

For a moment the young man looked at her in silence, and then he said :

"Why are you so quiet, dear Daisy?"

"I am unwilling to alter the pose that has won your approbation," she said demurely. "Don't you think if I retained it long enough I might 'be struck so,' as the man in *Patience* says?"

"I should be inclined to discourage that idea," said Alan, "as I was about to ask you to draw your seat a little nearer, and transfer your hands from the chair's arms to my head. You know I always liked you to run your long fingers through and through my hair. Have you forgotten how you used to do it? I can assure you I have not."

As Margaret made no answer, he went on:

"You were quite a child when you used first to do it—a tall little maid, even then, with such imperious ways! But you were always willing to do anything for your big boy cousin, and he has never forgotten you. All the time he was at college, and afterward, when he went abroad and travelled about in many strange and distant places, he carried with him always the image of that little maid, and when, at last, he turned homeward, one of his pleasantest visions was that of meeting her again."

Margaret had changed her position and turned more directly toward him; she was looking straight into his eyes, with her direct and candid gaze, which his own met rather dreamily. She did not speak in answer to these fond assurances of his, but as she listened she smiled.

"And are you glad to hear that I have always had this *tendre* for my sweet cousin, which I somehow can't get over, even yet?"

"Oh yes," said Margaret, gently, "very glad," and she looked at him with a deep and searching gaze, which he could not quite understand.

"Come nearer, dear," he said, "and take your old place at my head, and try to twist my short locks into curls, as you used to do. You will discover a secret known only to myself and the discreet fraternity of barbers. Come and see!" and he extended a white hand, somewhat languidly, to draw her toward him.

"I think not," said Margaret, drawing herself upright, into an attitude of buoyant self-possession. "You and the barbers may keep your secret, for the present. I won't intrude."

"Ah, but I want you. Come!" he said urgently, still holding out the delicate hand, on which a diamond sparkled.

But Margaret shook her head.

"Consider," she said, with a little smile; "hadn't I better stay where I am and pose for you, 'talking platitudes in stained-glass attitudes,' than put myself there, out of sight, encroaching upon the barbers' privileges in more ways than one? As there is only one of me, I think you had better let me stay where I am. There ought to be five or six—one at your Sereneness' head, and another at your feet. Two with jingling anklets and bangles, to dance in that space over yonder, and two just back of them, to discourse sweet music on their 'cith-erns and citoles'!"

Decourcy smiled at her banter, but he fancied he discerned in her voice a faint ring of earnestness, tinctured with scorn, that disconcerted him.

"What is the use of six," he said, "when I have the sweet ministrations of all, merged into one?—the little maid of long ago! Her comforting offices are an old experience, and, without having seen her dance, I'm willing to pit her against any pair of houris in the Orient; and as to music, I prefer the piano to citherns and citoles."

"Especially in the early morning hours," said Margaret, slyly, "when your Sereneness is enjoying your nap."

"Who told you anything about that?" he said, starting, and turning toward her abruptly.

"I guessed the truth and asked Amy, and she had to own it."

"I don't hear you in the least, where I am now. I hope you have not given up your practising on my account. I am afraid you have!"

" On the contrary," answered Margaret, " my effort is to make more noise, and I constantly use the loud pedal. If my instrument had been as movable as your apartment, I should have followed you across the hall."

" Why do you talk to me like this, Daisy? "

" Because I think you ought to come down in time for breakfast, and not give Amy the trouble of having things prepared afresh for you."

" Amy likes it," he said, smiling.

" It is very fortunate, if she does," said Margaret; "but I fancy she would do it all the same, whether she liked it or not. Amy never thinks of herself."

At this moment, Mrs. Guion entered, having at last soothed her little patient to sleep. Her first act was to bring a light screen and put it before her brother's face, to shield it from the fire.

" Amy, why will you? " said Margaret. " You spoil Alan frightfully. He's badly in need of discipline."

"I wish you would take me in hand," he said, looking at her from behind the screen with an eager expression, that disconcerted her.

Mrs. Guion's entrance introduced new topics, and the *tête-à-tête* between the cousins was not renewed.

The next morning being rainy, Margaret betook herself, after breakfast, to the little up-stairs apartment which was the children's general play-room, and as the three little creatures gathered around her, she drew Amy to her side and asked her to tell her what she thought of Baltimore on serious consideration.

"I don't like it one bit, Auntie Mard'ret," said Amy. "I think it's a nasty, hateful, dirty place."

"Why, Amy!" said Margaret, reproachfully, "I am shocked at your using such words. Where did a sweet little girl like you ever hear such bad words?"

"Oh, Auntie Mard'ret, I know a dreat deal worse words than that," said Amy, with her eyes opened very wide. "Why, if I was to tell you the words I'm thinkin' of, why you'd jump up and wun out of the woom."

"Amy, I must insist upon your telling me," said Margaret, feeling in duty bound to restrain her amusement, and administer the rebuke. "What words do you mean?"

"Oh, Auntie Mard'ret," said Amy, solemnly, "they's jes' is bad is they kin be—*awful* words! I couldn't never tell you."

Margaret insisted that she must be told, and after much reluctance on Amy's part, and a demanded banishment of Ethel and Dee to the other end of the room, she put her arms around her cousin's neck, and whispered in awe-struck, mysterious tones:

"I was thinkin' of *devil* and *beast*."

Margaret caught the little creature in her arms and kissed her repeatedly, in the midst of such a merry outburst of laughter as made reproof impossible.

Amy, who seemed greatly relieved to have rid her conscience of this burden, without any

penance in consequence, ran off to play with
the other children, and Margaret had just cut
the leaves of a new magazine she had brought
up with her and begun to look over the illustrations, when she became aware of a commo-
tion among the children at the other end of
the room and a confusion of excited voices.
Presently little Decourcy came running toward her in much perturbation, and said, with
a rising sob:

"Auntie Mard'rit, is I a bullabulloo? Amy
says I'se a bullabulloo. Now, is I?"

"No, Dee," said Margaret, soothingly, "you
are no such thing. Tell Amy I say you are
not."

Dee ran back to the closet, on the floor of
which Amy was seated dressing her doll, and
Margaret heard him say, triumphantly:

"Auntie Mard'rit says I'se not no bullabulloo."

Amy, taking a pin out of her mouth to fasten
the insufficient scrap of ribbon which she had
been straining around her daughter's clumsy
12

waist, looked up into his face with great, serious eyes, and said mysteriously :

" Yes, Dee, you *are* a bullabulloo. Auntie Mard'rit don't know it, and you don't know it; *but you are.*"

This idea was so hopelessly dreadful that poor little Dee could control himself no longer. He dropped his apronful of blocks upon the floor, and burst into a howl of despair.

Margaret flew to the rescue, and, lifting him in her arms, carried him off to the window, muttering soothing denials of his remotest connection with bullabulloos. When he was in some slight measure comforted, Margaret called Amy to her and rebuked her sternly for teasing her little brother. What was her amazement to see Amy, as soon as she had finished, look up at her with the same serious gaze, and say, gravely :

" Auntie Mard'rit, he *is* a bullabulloo. You don't know it, and Dee don't know it; but *he is.*"

At this poor Dee began to howl again, refusing to be comforted, until it occurred to Margaret to suggest that if he was a bullabulloo Amy must be one, too, as she was his sister. This idea, once mastered, proved consoling, and Dee stopped crying. Margaret, to try to banish the remembrance of his trouble, turned him around to the window and called his attention to the children next door, who were running about the back yard in the rain and apparently enjoying it immensely. Ethel and Amy had joined them at the window, the latter standing on tip-toe to look.

"That's Jack and Cora," she said, still grasping her doll with one arm, while she held on to the window-ledge with the other. "Oh, Auntie Mard'rit, they're such awful bad children. They don't mind their mamma nor nuthin'. You jes' ought to see how bad they are. I jes' expeck they'll all grow up to be Yankees."

Margaret burst into a peal of laughter.

"What makes you think they'll grow up to

be Yankees, Amy?" she said. "Did anybody ever tell you so?"

"No, Auntie Mard'rit, but they're so awful bad; and if they're that bad when they're little, I bet they *will* grow up to be Yankees."

At this point Mrs. Guion entered, and Margaret related the story to her with great zest.

"How *do* you suppose they got hold of such an idea?" she said.

"I can't imagine," said Mrs. Guion, "I'm sure they never got it from me. Alan will insist that they did, as he considers me a most bigoted rebel. But certainly I have never taught any such sentiment as that to the children. They must simply have imbibed it with the air they have breathed."

"It's an excellent story," said Margaret, laughing over it still; "I shall have no rest until I have told it to Mr. Gaston."

CHAPTER XII.

EVER since Mrs. Gaston had called attention to the fact that Alan Decourcy had a habit of watching her, Margaret had been conscious that it was really the case. He always listened attentively when she spoke, applauding by eloquent looks and smiles when her sentiments pleased him, and looking annoyed and disappointed when they did not. She could not help seeing that he was studying her with a deliberateness she felt somewhat inclined to resent.

It was hard to cherish any feeling of resentment against him, however, during that pleasant week in Baltimore, for he was kindness itself, contributing in every possible way to her comfort and enjoyment. Every night there was something pleasant going on, and Alan was always at hand, to act as escort, if no one else held the place. Margaret was delighted

with Baltimore, and when she expressed herself to this effect, Mr. Decourcy showed such
manifest approval of the sentiment that she
half regretted it the next minute. She was
beginning to feel a little disconcerted by certain signs she saw in Alan.

This young lady got so much pleasure and
entertainment out of everything, that it often
surprised her to catch glimpses of a carefully
concealed *ennui* in the expression of her
cousin's guarded countenance.

"I should not like to be as thoroughly
initiated as you are, Alan," she said to him one
day. "You've seen and done pretty much
everything, I suppose, and nothing has any
particular zest for you now."

"You audacious young fledgeling!" exclaimed her cousin. "How dare you make me
out such a *blasé* old fellow? How old am I, do
you suppose?"

"I really don't quite know."

"I am just barely thirty-three—not entirely
superannuated yet!"

"About three years older than Mr. Gaston!" said Margaret, reflectively.

"I can't understand the inflection of your voice," said Alan, rather eagerly; "do I seem that much older than he?"

"I hardly know," answered Margaret, still in the same thoughtful tone. "Mr. Gaston is such a busy man that he bears the impress of cares and responsibilities, and that makes him seem older; but in his feelings he seems worlds younger than you."

"And haven't I cares and responsibilities too, I'd like to know! Wait till I'm fairly launched in my profession, and see how I will peg away at my briefs and documents."

"Oh, Alan!" said Margaret, smiling indulgently, in a way that irritated him; "it is impossible to imagine you really at work. Have you ever practised at all?"

"Not yet. Circumstances have prevented, and I remained abroad much longer than I had any idea of doing; but one thing after another detained me. After Christmas, however,

I am going to open an office and go to work in earnest."

He spoke with confidence, but his tone did not impose upon his cousin, who in her heart had but small belief in his work. The fact was becoming more and more evident to her, that the nomadic life this elegant young gentleman had led had held him back from strong purposes, however much it had advanced him in social accomplishments and graces.

"If a man has done nothing, from choice, up to thirty," she said to herself, reflectively, "the chances are that, if the power of choice remains, he will continue to do nothing."

"I am so glad you are pleased with Baltimore, Margaret," said her cousin, interrupting her reverie. "How do you think you should like it as a residence?"

"Oh, I should like my home, wherever it chanced to be," said Margaret. "It is people, and not places, that make one's happiness, I think. I am sure I could be happy wherever my dear father and mother were."

"But you cannot have them always. By-and-by some one must take their place."

"Yes," said Margaret, "I suppose so, but I try not to think of that."

"Do you never think of marriage, Margaret? I suppose all young ladies must."

"Not often, as applied to myself," she said.

"Don't you think matrimony desirable?"

"I really don't know," said Margaret, a little uneasily. "Not as we usually see it, certainly. I suppose under the very best conditions marriage is the happiest life—but I know nothing about it."

"I am quite sure it is the happiest life," said Alan, "for both men and women, and it is the greatest possible mistake to put it off too long. Don't be too fastidious as to conditions, Margaret, and too high-flown in your notions. Mutual liking and respect, and congeniality of tastes are a good enough foundation—the rest will follow. A cheerful disposition is an immense consideration, and that you have. You will always make the best of whatever comes.

I don't think I ever saw a woman better fitted for matrimony."

He spoke so earnestly and looked at her with such intentness, that Margaret felt herself somewhat ill at ease, and was relieved when the door burst open and Decourcy came running in.

"Auntie Mard'rit, Ethel says you're not my really auntie," he said, wofully; "you is, now—ain't you, Auntie Mard'rit?"

"I love you just the same as if I were, Dee," said Margaret, lifting him to her knee. "I couldn't be your real auntie, you know, because I'm not your mother's or your father's sister. Can you understand that?"

"But Mrs. Gregg is Jack and Cora's auntie," said Amy, who had come to take part in the discussion, "and she's not their mamma's sister or their papa's either; she only married their uncle."

"And if Margaret married your uncle, she would be your really auntie, too," said Alan, quietly. "She could settle the whole matter,

if she would, and don't you think she might?
I do."

"Oh! Auntie Mard'rit, won't you please
marry uncle?" cried Amy, imploringly, while
Dee, partially seizing the idea, repeated
faintly :

"Auntie Mard'rit, peese marry uncle."

"Run away, children," said Margaret, provoked to feel herself blushing. "Alan, how
can you put such nonsense into their heads?"

"I am afraid it is but too true that you consider it nonsense," he said, with a gravity that
surprised her. Immediately afterward he left
the room, and Margaret found herself alone
with the children, who insisted on pushing
the question to its remotest issue with a per-
sistency that was almost distracting.

After this it was impossible but that she
should realize that her cousin was studying
her with a purpose. She could hardly suppose
that he thought seriously of asking her to
marry him, and yet the interest he displayed
in trying to direct her opinions pointed that

way. She made a strong effort to shake off the idea. Its deliberateness shocked her. Charming as her cousin was, his calm philosophicalness often irritated her, and she was at times inclined to believe him cold-blooded and selfish, until perhaps, just afterward, some act of kindness to herself or his sister or the children made her heartily ashamed of this suspicion. And, indeed, it was an easy thing to judge Alan Decourcy kindly. So he kept his place as a trusty and beloved kinsman.

Shortly before the end of Margaret's allotted week in Baltimore, Mrs. Gaston forwarded to her an invitation to a large party to be given by some people who happened to be friends of Alan Decourcy also, and insisted that both of them should come over in time for the entertainment. Margaret's week would be out, she said, and no extension of leave would be granted. So she was to come without fail, and to bring Mr. Decourcy with her. Alan readily acquiesced in the arrangement, and at the proper time they set forth together.

Margaret was feeling particularly well-disposed toward her cousin that afternoon, as they steamed along in the express train together. She had the recollection of a host of kind acts toward herself stored away in her mind, and it seemed to come almost more naturally than usual to her to like this pleasant, considerate, affectionate cousin.

When they had reached Washington, and were driving swiftly along the smooth asphalt pavements in Cousin Eugenia's snug coupé, Margaret said, cordially:

"You've done *everything* to make my visit a happy one, Alan! I do thank you so much."

"It has been a happy time to me," he said; "*so* happy! How capitally we get on together, Daisy—don't we?"

"It always makes me think of dear papa to hear you call me Daisy," answered the girl, instinctively avoiding a direct answer to his appeal. "I had forgotten that you called me so."

"I have adopted it intentionally," he said.

"Margaret seems cold, and I want to get rid of the sense of distance between us which our long separation has engendered, for who knows but by-and-by what you are pleased to call nonsense now may come to look differently, as use familiarizes it? Don't turn upon me in that sudden way, dear. I wouldn't startle you for the world. I only want you to promise to think of me often, until after a while I come to see you down in Bassett, and we can talk things over quietly and calmly."

"I shall always think of you as a kind and dear cousin," answered Margaret.

"But I cannot promise I shall always be content with that," he said, bending toward her, with a motion of great gentleness, and softly laying his gloved hand over hers. "My sweet Margaret," he murmured; "my strong hope is, that some day I can teach you to think of me as I would have you. And, meantime, I can wait."

Margaret made an effort to withdraw her hand, but he held it in a close, detaining clasp, and, looking up, she met his eyes fixed on her, with a gaze so sweet and tender, that it somehow seemed to soothe, while it agitated her. Once more she attempted to withdraw her hand, and this time he released it, but before doing so he raised it to his lips and kissed it.

Margaret felt deeply disturbed. It was something very new to her to see this phase in her cousin's relationship toward her, and the very fact that she felt in her heart no response to these signs of tenderness, distressed her. She knew the time must come when she would have to deny and thwart him, and the idea gave her pain. If she had hitherto doubted that he really loved her, she doubted it no longer. That look of his, as he lifted her hand to kiss it, made doubt impossible. It was no cool, cousinly affection; it was a passionate emotion that looked out from his eyes.

She felt relieved when the carriage stopped at General Gaston's door, and Alan, after handing her out, took leave, to be driven to his hotel to dine and dress. The remembrance of that look of his would not be shaken off, however, and she appeared before Mrs. Gaston in a somewhat pensive mood.

Cousin Eugenia was delighted to see her, and declared she had missed her unendurably. She informed her, hurriedly, that they were all well, and that Louis was in New York, having been there ever since the day after her own departure for Baltimore ; and then they fell to discussing Margaret's costume for the party.

" My white silk is all ready," said Margaret, somewhat listlessly. "I have not worn it yet, you know. It is high, and perhaps better suited to a dinner, but I like it, and suppose it will do."

" That splendid old lace would make it elegant enough for any occasion," said Mrs. Gaston ; " and as to the high neck, somehow that style suits you, in spite of the eminent presentability of your neck and arms. But go now to your room and take a good nap. Ring for a cup of tea when you get up. I want you to look very fresh to-night."

When Margaret entered her apartment, she caught sight of a letter on her dressing-table, and immediately her brows contracted. She knew the hand. It was from Charley Somers, and, to tell the truth, this young gentleman was somewhat in disgrace. He had some friends in Washington, and, a short time back, he had written to Margaret to ask her to allow him to come on and see her, with the ostensible purpose of visiting these friends. Margaret had written at once, and distinctly forbidden him to come. The mere suggestion made her indignant. It had the air of asserting a claim when no shadow of such existed. She supposed she had finally settled the matter, and what had he to say in this letter? She tore it open hastily and ran her eyes down the length of its pages; when she reached the end she threw it from her, with a motion of angry indignation. Mr. Somers wrote to say that the tone of her letter had made him feel so uneasy that, even at the risk of incurring her displeasure, he was coming on to Washington.

13

Margaret hastily pulled out her watch. There was yet time to catch the Southern mail. She threw off her hat and wraps, and sitting down at her desk scratched off a few hurried lines, saying to Mr. Somers, that he might come to Washington or not, exactly as it suited his pleasure, but forbidding him, in plain terms, to call upon her in the event of his doing so. Without pausing to read it over, she addressed and sealed the letter, and rang for a servant to post it.

CHAPTER XIII.

WHEN Miss Trevennon, dressed for the ball, descended to join her cousin that memorable December evening, she looked undeniably lovely, and so Mrs. Gaston admitted to herself with supreme satisfaction. The young girl's tall beauty was superbly displayed by this rather severe costume—with its heavy, gleaming drapery falling about her, white and plain. The flounces of rich lace made a splendid trimming for the long skirt, which trailed behind her in a graceful, shimmering mass, and the pointed body outlined to perfection her round and pliant waist. The dress was cut high, and a fall of the lovely lace finished the throat and sleeves.

Miss Trevennon's clear-cut, soft-tinted face was somewhat inanimate this evening. The ball had lost much of its charm since she had contemplated the prospect in the morning.

In the first place, the possibility of Charley Somers coming to Washington troubled her, and, in the second, Alan Decourcy's words and looks, with a chance of their repetition this evening, made her uneasy. Besides these, there was a feeling of disappointment, all the keener for being unowned, even to herself, that Louis Gaston should not be here to welcome her back, and to share the interest and pride Cousin Eugenia so evidently took in her appearance at this ball.

Arrived at their destination, Mrs. Gaston and Margaret, escorted by General Gaston, were passing through the main hall on their way to the dressing-rooms, when they came upon Alan Decourcy, with a sumptuously apparelled lady on his arm. She was a decidedly pretty woman, and Margaret observed that she clung to her companion with an air of the friendliest familiarity. She also observed that her pink gauze costume was somewhat *decolleté,* and that a strap of black velvet stood in lieu of a sleeve across her white shoulder, a similar bit supporting a superb pendant of diamonds, which ornamented her fair, round throat.

This lady bowed affably to Mrs. Gaston, and regarded Margaret with a broad stare. Alan, of course, spoke also, but for some reason Margaret avoided doing more than just glancing at him as she passed on toward the staircase.

"And so Mrs. Vere already has your cousin in her toils!" said Mrs. Gaston, as they were approaching the dressing-room.

"Was that Mrs. Vere?" said Margaret. "Who is she?"

"Oh, she's one of the most noted of the married belles!" said Mrs. Gaston. "If Mr. Decourcy were not a man of the world and well able to take care of himself, it might be well for you to warn him. As it is, I feel no anxiety about him."

"And who is Mr. Vere?"

"Mrs. Vere's husband. He may or may not be here. He's apt to turn up in the supper-room."

Margaret said no more, but set herself to the adjustment of her toilet with a certain air of preoccupation. Having ascertained by a glance that her costume was in order, she stood looking very thoughtful as she waited for her cousin, whose touches here and there consumed a much longer time.

When the two ladies emerged from the dressing-room together, they found Alan Decourcy, with General Gaston, awaiting them. He had freed himself from Mrs. Vere, in some way, and offered his arm to take Margaret into the room. She laid her hand within it lightly and they followed General and Mrs. Gaston in silence.

After they had spoken to their hostess and her daughters, Decourcy led Miss Trevennon away to make the tour of the rooms, which were ablaze with lights and flowers, and gorgeous to behold.

" There's something very distinguished about this dress you are wearing, Margaret," he said, in a tone that was caressingly sweet, "or is it, perhaps, my cousin's lovely face and figure that make it appear so? You are looking your very best, yet I never saw you so devoid of color."

"It's the contrast with Mrs. Vere's gorgeousness, perhaps!" said Margaret, with a rather strained little laugh. "When did you meet Mrs. Vere, by-the-way?"

He turned suddenly, and looked at her with a glance of keen scrutiny, but, seeing the utter unsuspiciousness of her frank gaze, he said carelessly:

"Mrs. Vere? Oh, she's a very old friend! I hardly remember the time when I didn't know Antoinette Vere."

"Did you know of her being in Washington?"

"Yes, indeed; I saw her when I was in town, the other day. She lives here."

"Why, I wonder you did not tell me you had this great friend living here, and make her come to see me!" said Margaret, in her honest way.

"I didn't think of it," he said, somewhat constrainedly. "I didn't suppose you'd care for it."

He turned, then, and called her attention to some especially pretty bit of decoration, and Mrs. Vere was not mentioned again.

In a few minutes Mr. Leary came up to speak to Miss Trevennon, and, soon after, one or two other acquaintances appeared, and Margaret was importuned for dances.

"I shall not dance this evening," she said, forming the resolution suddenly. She had not thought of the matter before, but when the time came she found herself indisposed to dance. There were strong protests from the young gentlemen, but these her decided manner soon silenced, and when Mr. Leary offered his arm, to take her to look for a seat, she looked around for Decourcy and found that he was gone.

For a long while after this, she had not time to think of her cousin. Scores of people were presented to her, by Mrs. Gaston and others,

and the General whispered to her that his
popularity with the young gentlemen this
evening was something phenomenal. She
went into the drawing-room and looked on for
a while, and though she kept to her resolution
she might have had two partners for every
dance, if she had chosen. Most of the men
whom she declined to dance with manifested
an entire willingness to stop and talk instead,
and throughout the evening she was so well
attended, that Cousin Eugenia, who had heard
with quaking of her resolution not to dance,
admitted to herself, in the end, that it had
given her young cousin a more distinguished
appearance.

When the evening was growing old, and the
flowers began to droop and the music to flag;
when the girls began to look the worse for too
much dancing, and the men, in many cases, the
worse for too much wine, Miss Trevennon, finding herself a little weary, yielded to the suggestion of her companion for the moment, who
happened to be Lord Waring, and allowed her-

self to be led to a cool, dim recess in the conservatory, where she sank into a seat to wait, while Lord Waring went for a glass of water for her. It was very still and quiet here. Almost every one was occupied either in the supper-room or in dancing, and Margaret supposed herself to be quite alone, until the sound of low-toned voices arrested her attention. Turning, she caught sight, between the branches of some densely leaved palms, of the figures of a man and woman. The latter's back was turned, but Margaret recognized the pink costume and smooth, bare shoulders. The head was raised to meet the ardent gaze of the man who bent above her. This man's face was turned full toward Margaret, and she, too, could see that gaze—a tender, fervid look that, but a few hours since, had been bent upon herself. Instinctively she closed her eyes, afraid to look longer, and feeling a quick pang of horror as she remembered that so recently this man had kissed her hand. Thank Heaven he had never, for one instant, touched her heart—that she cared not an atom for him! But suppose it had been different! Suppose the tenderness he had so successfully counterfeited, the significant words she had so implicitly believed, had awakened an answering tenderness in her heart!

As these hurried thoughts rushed through her mind, she rose to her feet, confused and agitated. Again her troubled gaze rested for one instant upon another vision of those two figures through the vista of flowers and leaves, but it was for an instant only, for she felt a swift instinct of flight, and forgetting Lord Waring and the fact that he would expect to find her where he had left her, she fled from the conservatory and entered the room beyond. Bewildered, agitated, weak, uncertain, she looked about her with a troubled gaze, and met the steadfast eyes of Louis Gaston.

With a look of joyful relief she hastened toward him and placed her hand, with a confiding motion, within the arm he extended. His

calm and self-collected aspect, the firm sup-
port of his strong arm, the repose of his quiet
manner, the freshness of his evening toilet,
recently made, which contrasted so pleasantly
with the somewhat dishevelled and flushed appearance of many of the men at this late hour,
all these were so restful and reassuring that
Margaret drew a long breath of contentment
to find herself so safe.

"Where did you come from?" she said.
"You were the very last person I expected to
see."

"I returned from New York by the evening
train, and, late as it was, I concluded to dress
and come to the ball. I have seen my hostess,
who has kindly forgiven my tardiness, and my
next thought was to find you. I was in the act
of seeking you in the supper-room when you
unexpectedly appeared before me, solitary and
alone."

"I was *so* glad to see you," she said, with
the unconscious simplicity a child might have
shown.

He took her words as naturally as they were uttered, and said simply :

" How did you happen to be alone ? "

" Oh, Lord Waring was with me," she said, suddenly, remembering her errant knight. " He went to get me some water. I wonder where he is."

At this moment Lord Waring appeared at the door of the conservatory, glass in hand.

Margaret hurriedly made her apologies, explaining her having caught sight of Mr. Gaston unexpectedly, his recent return from New York, etc.

His lordship accepted her explanation in good part, and when Margaret had drunk the water rather eagerly he went off to return the glass, saying he would see her again.

He had scarcely disappeared when Gaston and Margaret, going out into the hall, saw Mrs. Vere and Alan Decourcy coming toward them.

Gaston suddenly stood still, detaining his companion by a slight pressure of the arm, and said, hurriedly :

"It is just possible that Mrs. Vere may ask you to join a theatre-party she is getting up for to-morrow evening. Forgive me if I take the liberty of suggesting that you shall decline if she should do so. Make an engagement to go with me instead, and just excuse yourself on the plea of a previous engagement. I hope you will pardon my venturing to advise you."

"Certainly," said Margaret; "but she will not ask me. I do not know her."

Mrs. Vere, however, was coming straight toward them, and she now stopped in front of them, and giving Louis a tap with her fan, said:

"Present me to Miss Trevennon," and when Gaston had complied, she went on in a rather boisterous tone:

"I've been teasing your cousin to present me to you all the evening, Miss Trevennon; but I suppose he wanted the monopoly of you, for he would not even bring me into your neighborhood."

"It may have been that he wanted the

monopoly of yourself," said Gaston, looking at her keenly and speaking in his quietest tones.

"Well, it's more than you'll ever want, then!" said Mrs. Vere, pertly; "so you can just keep yourself out of the matter."

"I have every intention of doing so, madam," said Gaston, gravely. "I know my place, and I value my peace of mind."

Mrs. Vere flashed a quick, vindictive glance at him, as he uttered these quiet words, and then turning to Margaret, she said:

"I want to ask you to join a little theatre-party I am giving to-morrow evening, Miss Trevennon. There will be eight of us, and we are going to see *As You Like It*, and have a little supper at my house afterward. Now don't say you have any other engagement."

"Unfortunately I must," said Margaret, conscious of the insincerity of the qualifying term, and yet too grateful to Louis for preparing her for this contingency to feel very contrite on account of it. "I have already pledged myself elsewhere."

"How tiresome!" said Mrs. Vere, darting a suspicious glance at Louis, which he met with imperturbable gravity. "By-the-way, I called on you while you were in Baltimore. I suppose you got my card."

And, without waiting for an answer, she moved away, on Decourcy's arm, saying, as if half involuntarily :

"I detest that man."

Decourcy, who was looking somewhat pre-occupied, made no answer, until she gave his arm a little jerk and said, with the petulance of a child :

"What's the matter with you ? Why don't you speak ? "

"What can I say, except that I feel deeply sorry for poor Gaston, and appropriately grateful that I do not happen to be in his place."

He spoke in his softest tones, but Mrs. Vere knew instinctively that her spell was, for the time being, broken. Well ! it had been broken before, she reflected, and she had always succeeded in mending it, and she felt confident she could do so again.

Meantime, as Margaret and Louis walked away, to look for Mrs. Gaston, the former said:

"Was it not rather odd that Mrs. Vere didn't ask you to join her party?"

"She did," said Louis. "She wrote me a note, which was forwarded to me in New York."

"And what did you do?" asked Margaret.

"Excused myself on the score of another engagement."

"But you didn't——" she began, and then stopped with uplifted eyebrows.

"I know," he answered, smiling; "but I foresaw at least the possibility that you would be propitious."

"I think she's angry with you about it."

"Very likely. She's been angry with me before."

"I didn't know, until to-night, that she was an old friend of Alan's," said Margaret.

"Oh yes," he answered, indifferently; "it's an affair of long standing, I hear."

14

"What do you mean?" said Margaret, facing him with a sudden surprise, and then, remembering the scene she had witnessed in the conservatory, she averted her eyes, and was silent.

"I merely meant," he answered, in a tone of quick regret, "that I happened to hear Waring say that they were friends in London, last year. Mr. and Mrs. Vere spent the season there, and your cousin happening to be there also, naturally saw them often—all being Americans together."

At this point they caught sight of Mrs. Gaston, and Margaret hastened to join her, and so the subject was very willingly dropped by them both.

Cousin Eugenia declared and reiterated that Margaret had been a shining success at this ball, but of that the girl thought and cared little. But for many days to come, the recurring thoughts of that evening brought with them certain memories that rankled, as well as certain others that comforted and soothed.

CHAPTER XIV.

"AND so Mrs. Vere wanted you in her theatre-party!" said Cousin Eugenia to Margaret, the next morning, as they were driving about in a flutter of preparation for Christmas. Margaret had sent off a charming box home, and she was now assisting Mrs. Gaston in the completion of her various Christmas schemes.

"Yes," she answered quietly, "and I declined."

"Louis told me about it. It's just as well you got out of it. He was afraid he had ventured too far in advising you. He said he felt he had no sort of right to do it, and that, in most cases, he should have held his peace; but he couldn't bear to think of you in the midst of Mrs. Vere's set, and he found the impulse to prevent it too strong to be resisted."

"He was quite right," said Margaret, feeling a little throb of pleasure in the considerate interest implied in what Mr. Gaston had said. "I should not have wanted to go, in any case, but I might not have known how to avoid it, and he gave me the means. I felt very thankful to him. But what is it that makes both you and Mr. Gaston distrust Mrs. Vere?"

Cousin Eugenia gave a little shrug.

"Mrs. Vere is extremely pretty," she said, "and of course she has admirers. She is certainly very free in her ways with them, but I know no more than that, and I certainly don't care to know more. I asked Louis why he objected to your going with her, and he said, with that frown of his, that you could not possibly find any pleasure in her acquaintance. He would say nothing more, but I felt sure, by the way he looked, that there was a good deal kept back."

"I wonder at Alan Decourcy," said Margaret.

"Do you?" said Mrs. Gaston. "I don't.

I have long since ceased to wonder at any man's admiring any woman."

"But how can he? He is so fastidious."

"Perhaps I used the wrong word," said Mrs. Gaston; "to admire a woman is one thing and to find her amusing is another. I fancy Mr. Decourcy finds Mrs. Vere amusing—most men do, indeed—and your cousin is the sort of man with whom that is paramount. With men of a certain type the woman who can furnish them most amusement will ever have the strongest hold upon them, and to that type I rather think your fascinating cousin belongs. As I said, most men find Mrs. Vere amusing, and as her husband does not look after her at all, the coast is clear for them to come and be amused; and they come."

"I don't think Mr. Gaston finds her amusing," said Margaret.

"Louis! I should think not!" said Mrs. Gaston, warmly. "My dear, you don't know Louis yet—perhaps you never will. Very few people besides Edward and I know what that boy is. I know him, through and through, and I unhesitatingly declare that he's an angel. I believe he's of a different grain from other men. Mrs. Vere could no more ensnare him than she could put shackles on a mist-cloud; and for that reason—because she knows her usual darts are powerless with him—she is feverishly anxious to get him in her toils. I'll do her the justice to say her efforts have been masterly. She's left no stone unturned. She's tried the musical dodge, and invited him to warble duets with her. That must have been a temptation, for you know how he loves music, and her voice is charming. She's tried the charity dodge, and has come to him with tears in her eyes to get him to make plans for cottages she proposed to erect for poor people on her estate in the outer antipodes. He told me about that himself, and what do you sup-pose was his answer to her appeal? He told her that when she had made arrangements with the builder to go to work, to tell the lat-ter to write to him on the subject and he would gladly furnish the plans for her cottages and feel himself honored in advancing her good work—begged her not to mention the question of payment, and bowed her out of his office with the assurance that the builder's letter should find him most willing to co-operate, and insisted that she should wash her fair hands of these dry business details and leave them entirely to the builder and himself. She plucked up courage on the landing, to tell him she had some plans to submit. He replied to this that, as he had long since submitted himself and all his designs and aspirations to his partner, and as he did not venture to call his soul, much less his squares and angles, his own, without the approbation of Mr. Ames, her plans must be submitted to the firm at New York, where he would promise to give them his circumspect attention under the judicious eye of his chief. It must have been a funny scene," said Cousin Eugenia, smiling. "Poor Mrs. Vere! She let him alone severely for some time after that, but she finally began

again on another tack. I think she is beginning to understand now that there is one man
who can resist her, and when once she is quite
persuaded that she is vanquished, how she
will hate him! There's nothing she wouldn't
do to avenge herself; but I fancy Louis is as
far beyond the range of her revenge as he is of
her fascination. The truth is, as to Louis,"
Cousin Eugenia went on, after a moment's
pause, " that he's radically cold-blooded. He's
affectionate to his friends and relatives, and
really fond of many of them, but he's absolutely unemotional—not to be roused to deep
feeling. But for this fact I fear Mrs. Vere's
efforts would have been long since crowned
with success. It is really a valuable trait for
a man to have, if it were only for its unique-
ness, but occasionally it's a little bit exasperating. Who but Louis, for instance, would have
lived all these weeks in the same house with a
charming girl like you without falling, at least
a little, in love with her? For you are a
charming girl, my dear, and Louis accurately

appreciates the fact; but there it ends. At first I thought I saw signs of a speedy capitulation, but it came to nothing. I ought to have known the frogginess of my brother-in-law better. I should have liked Louis to fall in love with you, no matter how it ended. It would have been nice to have you for a sister and neighbor, and if that was not to be, it would have been a satisfaction to see Louis stirred out of his eternal calm, and concerning himself about something over and above designs and estimates. But I am afraid I am never to have the supreme delight of seeing Louis love-lorn. And you, my dear," said Cousin Eugenia, turning to look at her, " I begin to fear you're not very far from being rather froggy yourself. It's a very good thing that you've taken no more of a fancy to Louis, as it all turns out—(I fancied you, too, were in some danger at first!)—but I do wonder how you have kept so cool about that captivating young man, your cousin, with his sweet, caressing smiles and artful, foreign ways. The Mrs.

Vere episode would have been rather a blow, I fear, if you had set your affections in that quarter."

"On the whole," said Margaret, smiling, "it seems to me that I am escaping a good many breakers by remaining fancy free. But here we are at our destination."

And so the conversation ended.

During this day—the one that followed the party—Margaret received a note from Charley Somers, bearing a Washington post-mark. Observing this, her first angry thought was to return it unopened, so indignant was she at his persistence, and when she presently decided to read it, its humble and imploring tone did not mollify her in the least. Her letter of course had not reached him, and he had grown impatient and concluded not to wait to hear from her.

She wrote him a few lines, declining explicitly to see him, feeling herself justified in taking so extreme a measure, as lesser ones had failed to repress the young man's ardor.

CHAPTER XV.

ON Christmas-eve, after dinner, as General and Mrs. Gaston, Miss Trevennon and Mr. Louis Gaston were seated around the drawing-room fire, a card of invitation was brought in by Thomas, and delivered to General Gaston. As he took it and scanned it through his glasses, a perceptible gleam of satisfaction came into his eyes, and he handed it to Mrs. Gaston, saying:

"A card for General Morton's supper."

"Indeed!" returned his wife, with a reflection of his gratified expression. "Really, this is very kind."

As she took the card and looked at it, Margaret surveyed her wonderingly. Turning her eyes away from her cousin's face, an instant later, she saw that Louis Gaston was regarding her with a sort of deprecating amusement. He was seated near to her, and so he alone dis-

tinguished her words, when she murmured, in
an undertone :

"'How strange are the customs of France'!"

She smiled as she said it, and Cousin Eugenia, who saw the smile, but missed the
words she had uttered, said explainingly :

"This supper of General Morton's is an an-
nual affair. He has given one on New Year's
night ever since he has been in Washington.
They are limited to twenty-five gentlemen, and
of course these are carefully selected. It is
always the most *recherché* stag-party of the season, and one is sure of meeting there the most
distinguished and agreeable people the city
will afford. He has always been so kind in
asking Edward, though of course the invitations
are greatly in demand, and residents cannot
always expect to receive them."

Nothing further was said about the matter
just then, but it was evident that this attention from General Morton had put Mrs. Gaston
in unusually high spirits, and her husband, on
his part, was scarcely less elated.

A little later, when Louis and Margaret happened to be alone, the former said :

"I wish you would tell me what it was that amused you about that invitation. The system of social tactics, of which you are the exponent, begins to interest me extremely. What was it that brought that puzzled look to your face just now ?"

"Shall I really tell ? " the girl asked, doubtfully.

"Pray do—frankly. I'm so interested to know."

"I was wondering who this General Morton could be, that a card to his supper should be deemed such an acquisition. I have discovered the fact that you Gastons are proud of your lineage, and, as I have heard it said that yours is one of the few really historical families of America, perhaps it should not be wondered at. Who then, can General Morton be, I was thinking, to be in a position to confer honor on the Gastons? I suppose he's some one very grand, but I'm such an ignoramus that I really don't know who the Mortons are, when they're at home."

"I believe Morton's origin was very common," said Louis. " Certainly, he has no sort of claim to aristocratic distinction. He has a high official position and is very rich and a very good-natured, sensible sort of man, but it is out of the question that he could, socially speaking, confer honor upon my brother."

"And yet it was evident," began Margaret— but she stopped abruptly, and Louis made no motion to help her out.

"Do you know," he said, presently, " that, through your influence, Miss Trevennon, I have been gradually undergoing certain changes in my points of view. I am getting an insight into your social basis and system, and, stubborn Yankee as I am, I must admit that there's something fine in it. I really think I begin to feel myself veering perceptibly. Until I met you, I had no idea what a difference there was between the Northern and Southern ideas of these matters."

"But I must not be taken as a strict representative of the Southern idea—nor you, I suppose, for a strict representative of the Northern idea," said Margaret. "At home, they think me a great radical. I have no special respect for pedigrees in general. That one's forefathers should have been honest is the first thing, it seems to me, and that they should have been social luminaries should come a long way after."

"You rather amaze me in that," said Louis. "I thought there were no sticklers for birth and ancestry like the Southerners."

"It is perfectly true of a large class of them," said Margaret; "but I have seen too much of the degeneration of distinguished families in the South, to have much sympathy with that idea. In too many cases they have lacked the spirit to save them from such degeneration, and, that being the case, what does their blood go for? It ought to go for nothing, I think—worse than nothing, for if it has any virtue at all, it should make its possessors independent and manly."

"You have sometimes sneered a little gentle sneer at the Gaston pride—have you not?" said Louis; "and I've sometimes thought it odd, because I had always been told that the pride of the Southern people is unprecedented."

"It is of a different sort," said Margaret; " for instance——"

But she checked herself, and colored.

"Oh, pray give me the example," said Louis, earnestly. "Illustrations are such helps. I beg you will not let any over-sensibility prevent your speaking plainly. It may be that you've got the best of these social questions. I want to be able to judge."

"How honest and fair you are!" said Margaret, "and how rare that spirit is! I really think I'll tell you frankly what I was going to say. You know what an appreciation of your brother I have, and how entirely his fine qualities command my respect, but I will not deny that his bearing in the matter of this invitation has amazed me. I think I am safe in saying that no Southern man, in your brother's sphere of society, could possibly be found—no matter how insulated or behind the times he might be —no matter how poor or incapable or ignorant, who could be agitated and flattered by an invitation from General Morton or General anybody else. The notion would never penetrate their brains. But I am very bold," she said, checking herself suddenly. " I am afraid I have said too much."

"It would be too much for any one else to say to me certainly," said Louis, looking steadily at her, " and I cannot say the idea you suggest is exactly palatable ; but I think I could hardly take offence at words of yours."

At that moment the door-bell rang, and presently Thomas announced General Reardon.

" Generals seem to be the order of the day," said Margaret, with a smile, as the visitor was crossing the hall. " I might be back in Bassett for the prevalence of titles."

Miss Trevennon greeted General Reardon

with great cordiality, and set herself at once
to the task of entertaining him. He called
only occasionally at the Gastons' house, as he
did not enjoy their society any more than they
did his. He had been in the United States
Army before the war, and had been extremely
popular among the officers, being possessed of
a fund of anecdote and humor, which congealed
instantly in the atmosphere of the Gastons'
drawing-room, but flowed freely enough in
camps and barracks. He was of a good Southern family, and essentially a gentleman. His
visits, as has been indicated, were not especially inspiring to the Gastons, but Cousin Eugenia had detected in her husband a faint
tendency to slight this distant cousin of hers,
and it was just like her, after that, to treat him
with greater distinction. General Gaston, in
truth, found it a little difficult to ignore the
fact that he was an officer in the Federal army
who had gone with the South, and certainly
did not enjoy his visits; but he stood in some
awe of his wife, which enabled him partially

to conceal the fact that he chafed under her cousin's companionship.

When Thomas had summoned his master and mistress to the drawing-room, Mrs. Gaston seated herself near General Reardon, and at once fell into fluent conversation with him. General Gaston, for his part, established himself half-way between this couple and the pair who were seated on the other side of the fire-place. He sat very straight and erect in his chair, occasionally making a rather forced remark to General Reardon, who, in his turn, was conscious of being bored and ill at ease, but entirely unconscious of being the object of any slight whatever. It occurred to him, perhaps, that his host's manner was peculiar, even unfortunate, but it would have taken a great deal to convey to his honest breast the suspicion that any gentleman alive could mean to slight a visitor in his own house.

Mrs. Gaston, when she chose, could talk agreeably to any one on almost any subject, and she was now discussing crops and market-gardening, and listening, with great vivacity of expression, to a detailed account that General Reardon was giving of the reports his wife—whom he called "Loose," her name being Lucy—related of the result of a little venture in the way of a market-garden which they had made.

"By-the-way, General," said the visitor, breaking off suddenly from his conversation with Mrs. Gaston, and turning to address her husband; as if struck with a sudden thought; "are you invited to this supper of General Morton's?"

Imperceptible bristles began to rise over General Gaston's surface. He drew himself still more erect, and cleared his throat once or twice before answering.

"Ah—I beg your pardon—ah—yes," said General Gaston, with an inflection that suggested that he was rather asking a question than answering one. He cleared his throat again and went on, with a certain superciliousness that Margaret noted carefully. "General Morton has been kind enough to remember me and send me a card. There is always a very distinguished company at these suppers of his, and I shouldn't think of missing this."

"Loose wants me to go," responded General Reardon, in indolent, indifferent tones that set Margaret's blood a-tingling with delight; "but I don't care anything about it. I s'pose the men'll all wear swallow-tails, and I haven't got one. I'll tell Morton he'll have to let me off.— What I was going to tell you about the potato crop, is this," he said, returning to his conversation with Mrs. Gaston, as being the more interesting of the two. "Loose says, if we'd planted Early Rose——"

But Margaret listened no further. She knew Louis was looking at her, and she had drawn down the corners of her mouth, demurely, in her efforts not to laugh ; but her eyes brimmed over with such sparkling merriment, that the mouth's quiescence went for little.

Mr. Gaston presently drew out his watch, and reminded Miss Trevennon of the fact that it was nearly time to set out for the theatre, in fulfilment of their engagement, so she excused herself, and went to put on her wraps.

When the two young people found themselves alone together, in the clear, bracing atmosphere of the city streets—they had chosen to walk—Margaret began the conversation by saying :

" Alan Decourcy called while we were out driving this morning. I hope we shall not happen to be in view of the theatre-party to night ; it would be a little awkward, as we both refused to join it."

"Not at all," said Louis, " they need never know but that our engagement antedated their invitation. Don't give yourself any uneasiness about that."

When they had gone on a few moments in silence, Louis said in his pleasant voice, which even in the darkness indicated that he was smiling :

" Well, you had your little triumph this evening ! "

" I did," returned Margaret, with a soft, little

laugh, "and I must say I enjoyed it. But I was wondering how he happened to know General Morton."

"Oh, I dare say they were chums in the United States Army, before the war," said Louis. "Only think what a chance that man threw away! Why, if he had remained in the Union army he might have been a Major-General by this time."

"He is a Major-General, I think," said Margaret, demurely; "or is it only a Brigadier?"

"You impertinent little rebel!" said Louis. "How dare you say that to me? How do you know I will submit to such audacity? You make heavy draughts upon my clemency."

"I'm afraid I do," said Margaret; "but I've always had them generously honored. But while we are on the subject, there's one thing that I do want to say to you. Do you know, I have observed that your brother never gives General Reardon his title? In speaking of him to me or Cousin Eugenia, he always says 'your cousin,' and in speaking to him he

avoids calling him anything at all.   Once only,
when he had to say something, he called him
' Mr. Reardon.'   He did indeed ! "

" Well, in point of fact, you know," said
Louis, rather uncomfortably, " he's got no
more right to the title of General than you
have.   The point has been definitely decided.
It is only a matter of courtesy."

" I don't know who had the power to decide
it," Margaret said; " but we are not consider-
ing the point of legal right.   Its being, as you
admit, a matter of courtesy, should settle the
thing, I think.   Don't you ? "

" Yes," he said, " I do.   I'm not sure I always thought so, but I do now."

When they reached the theatre, they found
the overture just begun.   A few minutes later
they saw Mrs. Vere's party enter and place
themselves in their box.   The dashing young
hostess led the way, and seated herself *en évi-
dence*, with a brilliant party grouped about her.
One or two of these Margaret recognized, and
Louis knew them all, naming them, without

comment, to Margaret. There was some one whom they did not see, sitting in the shadow behind the curtain, and to this person Mrs. Vere directed a greater part of her attention. She constantly leaned to speak to him, or bowed her head to catch his utterances, casting toward him now and then the languishing looks which her peculiarly long eyelashes rendered so effective. Margaret felt that this person was Alan Decourcy, and at the end of the first act her suspicion was proved to be correct, as he then rose and came to Mrs. Vere's side to take a survey of the house. He looked very graceful and elegant, but, in some way, the great charm his appearance had once possessed for her was gone.

When she turned her eyes away from him, they rested, almost without any volition of her own, upon Louis Gaston's quiet profile. He was looking away from her, and so she could scan at leisure the earnest lineaments that had in them a genuineness and nobleness so much better than beauty. The more she felt her

disappointment in Alan Decourcy, the more
she believed in and rested upon Louis Gaston's friendship. Imperceptibly her regard
for him had widened and deepened, until now
merely to think of him was to feel peaceful and
safe and at rest.

CHAPTER XVI.

CHRISTMAS Day was fine and brilliant, and
Margaret awaked early. Her first thoughts
were of home and distant friends. How well
she knew that the dear father and mother, far
away in Bassett, were thinking of her! As she
rose and dressed, her heart was in full unison
with the day's sweet lesson of peace and good-
will, and when she knelt to say her morning
prayers, she had a vague feeling that somehow
this Christmas Day was a fuller and better one
than any she had known before. She did not
ask herself what was the new element in her
life that made it so; it was too indefinite to
be formulated into a tangible idea, but she felt
conscious of its presence.

General and Mrs. Gaston had a charming
present for her when she went down to breakfast—a pair of exquisite gold bracelets of the
most beautiful design and workmanship, and,

as they seemed really pleased with the little presents that she had prepared for them, they had a very satisfactory beginning of their Christmas Day. After breakfast, she went to her room to write a letter home, and when that was done it was time to dress for church.

A little before eleven, as Miss Trevennon was standing in the deep bow-window of the drawing-room, equipped for the morning service, she heard a firm tread on the carpet behind her, and the next moment her somewhat rusty little Prayer-book and Hymnal were slipped from her hand, and a marvellous tortoise-shell case, containing two beautiful little books, substituted for them. Margaret looked up quickly, and met Louis Gaston's smiling eyes. He had searched New York over for the prettiest set he could find, and the result satisfied him.

"You will use these instead, will you not?" he said. "I wanted to give you some little thing."

A flush of pleasure rose to Margaret's face.

"I never saw anything half so lovely," she

said, handling them delightedly. " To think of your taking the trouble! I suspect my shabby little books offended your fastidious taste. I never dreamed of your remembering me in this kind way. I wish I had a present for you."

"You might give me the old ones, perhaps," he said, hesitatingly. "I should think it a munificent return, for, as you say, they are worn and shabby, and that comes only from much using. How often they have been in your hands when your thoughts were away with God! I should like to keep them as a souvenir of you. May I, if you don't particularly value them ? "

"I should be only too glad for you to have them," said Margaret, in a low voice. "Only I did not think you would care for anything like that. I asked Cousin Eugenia once what church your family belonged to, and she said you called yourselves Unitarians, but practically you were pagans. I couldn't help hoping it was not really true—of you at least."

"It isn't in the least true of me," he said, frowning, and looking so displeased that Margaret was almost sorry she had spoken. "I would not, for anything, have you to suppose me an irreligious man, for it is not true, and I never even called myself a Unitarian. On the contrary, I was wishing a little while ago that I could go with you to church, so that you and I might keep this day holy together."

"Do," said Margaret, earnestly. "I have seen that you do not very often go. Go with us to-day, and make a resolve for better things in future. You would be so wise to do it."

"I don't think I will go this morning," he said; "Eugenia has not room for me in the coupé. But will you let me take you to-night? We will walk, perhaps, if it remains fine, and the music will be lovely. Perhaps, if we're lucky, they will get some good voice to sing the *Cantique de Noël*."

"I love that so dearly," Margaret said. "I shall be delighted to go with you."

A little sigh rose, as she spoke. This was

one of Charley Somers' favorites; she had taken pains to see that he sang it correctly, and his voice was trained to it beautifully.

Her reflections were cut short by the appearance of Mrs. Gaston, who swept down the steps, elaborately arrayed in furs and velvets, and signified her readiness to set out.

Louis helped them into the carriage, and then turned away, saying he was going for a long walk. There was a look of gravity on his face that Margaret found herself recalling long afterward.

The weather continued fine, and it proved quite mild enough for Louis and Margaret to walk to church in the evening. As they took their way along the gayly lighted streets, the young man turned suddenly and, looking down into her face, said:

"Do you know, I found a little pressed flower in my Hymnal, when I opened it this morning. Am I to keep it or return it to you?"

They were just under a gas-light, and Margaret, though she would not drop her eyes under his searching gaze, felt that she looked confused, as she said :

"No; you must give that back to me. I had forgotten it."

It was a little flower that Charley Somers had put in there one evening, and she had never happened to remove it.

Mr. Gaston put his hand into his pocket and took out the book. It opened easily at the place, and he removed the flower, which was run into a little slit, and handed it to her as they entered the church vestibule.

"There were some initials under it," he said.

"Oh, you can just rub those out. It doesn't matter," said Margaret, as she took the flower. She was about to crush and throw it from her, when a pang of pity for poor Charley checked her; so she opened her own Prayer-book and hurriedly slipped it among the leaves.

The service seemed wonderfully sweet to her that night. The hymns and anthems were triumphant and inspiring, and the sermon was simple, earnest and comforting. Louis found his places, and used his little book sedulously, and Margaret felt intuitively that this service was sweet to him also. As she glanced at him occasionally, she saw that his face looked serious and a little careworn, now that she saw it in such perfect repose.

The sermon was ended now. The congregation had risen at its termination, and had settled again in their seats. The wardens were walking up the aisle to receive the almsbasins, when the organ began to murmur a low prelude. Louis and Margaret glanced at each other quickly. It was the *Cantique de Noël.*

Margaret leaned back in her seat, serene and restful, prepared for a deep enjoyment of the pleasure before her, and at that moment a rich, sweet voice, high up in the choir behind her began :

" Oh, holy night—— "

At the first note uttered by that voice the color rushed to Miss Trevennon's cheeks, and

16

she drew in her breath with a sound that was almost a gasp.

And up on high the beautiful voice sang on :

"It is the night of the dear Saviour's birth."

Higher and sweeter it soared—thrilling, rich, pathetic—and how familiar to the young girl's ears was every modulation and inflection! How often had that flood of melody been poured forth, for her ear alone, in the old parlor at home!

It was Charley Somers, and she knew that he had seen her, and that he was singing to her now, no less than then. She listened, as in a dream, while the wistful, yearning voice sang on.   And now came the words :

"Fall on your knees ! fall on your knees !

They were somewhat indistinct, in their mingling of sweet sounds, and, in some vague way, it seemed to Margaret that they were a direct appeal from Charley Somers to her for mercy and pardon.

It was all so moving, and Gaston felt so touched by it himself, that it scarcely surprised him when he glanced at Margaret, as the sweet voice died away, to see that her eyes were full of tears. As they knelt for the concluding prayer she brushed away the traces of these, and when they walked down the aisle together her calmness had quite returned. And how calm and quiet her companion looked! His perfectly chosen clothes, the smooth neatness of his short, dark hair, and, more than all, his self-collected bearing and thoughtful face, made him a contrast to the rather carelessly dressed young man, with dishevelled, curly locks, and eager, restless eyes, who stood in the vestibule, at the foot of the gallery steps, rapidly scanning the faces of the dispersing congregation, in complete unconsciousness of the fact that his somewhat singular conduct and appearance were being observed by those around him. As his restless gaze at last fell upon Miss Trevennon, his knit brows relaxed, and he pressed forward.

"May I come to see you to-morrow?" he said, in eager tones, which, though low, were distinctly audible to Louis.

"Yes," replied Margaret at once, in a somewhat tremulous voice, "at eleven in the morning."

Then, taking her companion's arm, she passed on. Louis had observed that the two did not shake hands, nor exchange any word of greeting. This hurried question and answer was all that passed between them. What had there been in a short, casual meeting like that to make the girl look pale and excited, as her companion saw by a furtive glance that she was? He could feel her hand tremble slightly when she first laid it within his arm, but the little, almost imperceptible flutter soon ceased, and she walked on very quiet and still. And so they took their way along the streets in silence. She did not seem inclined to talk, and he would not jar her by speaking.

Margaret, as she mused upon this meeting, was blaming herself for the concession she had made, which was indeed attributable altogether to the music.

"I have no resolution or power of resistance whatever, when I'm under the influence of music," she said to herself, half angrily. "It takes away my moral accountability. I don't believe the story of the sirens is a fable. A beautiful voice could draw me toward itself as truly as the pole draws the magnet. It is intense weakness. I ought to have told him No, and ended the matter at once."

Remembering that her companion would have reason to wonder at her silence, Margaret roused herself with an effort and made some comment on the service.

"It was all very beautiful," said Louis. "I felt it very much, and I feel very happy to have gone. That solo was exquisitely sung. The voice does not seem to be highly cultivated, but it was thrillingly sweet."

"It was Mr. Somers, the young man from Bassett, whose voice I have spoken to you of. He has just come to Washington, and I knew he would want to see me, so I named an hour when I was sure to be free."

When they had reached home and were going up the steps, they found Thomas opening the door for a colored servant-man, who had two small parcels in his hand. He took off his hat and stepped back as they came up, and Thomas said :

"It is a parcel for Miss Trevennon."

Margaret turned and held out her hand for it.

"Where from ? " she said.

"From the Arlington, Miss," replied the man, in evident trepidation. "I'm very sorry, Miss, but there's been a mistake. It was to have been sent this morning, but it has been such a busy day that it has been forgotten. Mr. Decourcy left particular orders, and I hope you'll be kind enough to excuse the delay, Miss."

Margaret turned the parcel so as to get the light from the hall gas upon it. As she did so, her expression changed quickly. It was addressed to Mrs. Vere.

" There is some mistake," she said, coldly, with a certain high turn of the head that Louis knew. " This is not for me."

The poor negro, who was perhaps somewhat the worse for the wine remnants left by the Arlington's Christmas guests, was overwhelmed with confusion, and, quickly extending the other package, explained that he had made a mistake between the two, and asked Miss Trevennon rather helplessly to see if this one was not addressed to herself.

It proved to be so; and though, under the circumstances, Margaret would have preferred not to touch it, she was compelled to take it and dismiss the man, which she did somewhat curtly.

She did not examine her parcel until she reached her own room, and even then she tossed it on the bed, and removed her wraps and hat and put them away before she untied the string which bound it. Once she thought she would put it out of sight until to-morrow, but, despite her disfavor toward the giver, she had a young lady's natural curiosity as to the gift, and so she presently took it up and untied it. A little note fell out. It was dated Christmas morning at nine, and ran:

"I am just leaving for Baltimore, under a pledge to spend to-day with Amy and the children. I have been more than disappointed—*hurt* at missing you, both when I called and at the theatre last evening. I did not know you had been present, until I heard it by accident, after we had left. It had not at all entered into my calculations to forego the pleasure of taking leave of you in person, and I propose to get the better of fate by returning in a day or two for this purpose.

"Merry Christmas, dear Daisy, and all good wishes for the coming year! Who knows what it may have in store for us?

"Wear my little present sometimes for the sake of yours devotedly, A. D."

"So much for note number one!" said Margaret. "It would be interesting to have a glance at note number two, which I have no doubt is equally tender and gracious."

She took up the little leather case and opened it, revealing a beautiful locket. In spite of herself, she could not withhold a tribute to her cousin's taste. The workmanship and design of this little ornament were so effective and so uncommon that she felt sure Alan must have gone to some trouble about it, and most likely had it made expressly for her.

"He *is* kind," she said, regretfully. " It *was* good of him to go back to Baltimore, in order that Amy and the children should not be disappointed. I almost wish I had not made this new discovery about him; but no, no, no! It would have been dreadful to be ignorant of the real truth of the matter."

It occurred to her now to open the locket and, on doing so, her cousin's high-bred face looked out. The very sight of it made her recoil inwardly. How well she remembered the look of these same eyes, as they had been bent upon Mrs. Vere, with an expression she would have liked to forget. What right had he to expect her to wear his picture ? Why should she ?

He had sent another note and another present elsewhere. Was there another picture, which some one else had been gracefully urged to wear, for the sake of hers devotedly ? It was more than probable !

"I half believe I begin to understand him," she said to herself, indignantly. "It is one of his sage and correct opinions that a man should marry, but all the same a man wants his little diversions. Under these circumstances he had better marry an amiable, easy-going young thing, who is healthy and cheerful, who knows nothing of the world, and who will leave him to pursue his little diversions undisturbed. It is perfectly humiliating! I will return his locket, for the very sight of it would always sting me."

CHAPTER XVII.

MR. SOMERS came promptly at eleven, the
next morning, and Margaret received him
in the drawing-room alone. She had given orders that she should be denied to any early visitors who might be coming in, and was resolved
that she would be just and patient with the
young man, though she was also resolved that
the nature of their relationship should be
definitely settled and understood, during this
interview.

They had not been seated long when Margaret heard Louis Gaston's voice speaking to
a servant in the hall. She looked up in surprise, as she had supposed him to be at his
office an hour ago. He came in, with his overcoat on, and his hat in his hand, and when
Margaret presented him to Mr. Somers he cordially offered him his disengaged hand. Margaret was struck with the contrast between the

two general exteriors, as she had been the night before, but she was not a whit ashamed of her old friend. She told herself that no man with eyes in his head could fail to see that Somers was a gentleman, and, for the rest, it did not matter.

"I learned from my sister-in-law," said Louis, addressing Mr. Somers, "that Miss Trevennon was receiving a visit from a friend from home; and Mrs. Gaston has authorized me to come and engage you for dinner to-day, if you have no other appointment. I hope you will be able to come."

Margaret, glancing at Mr. Somers, was distressed to see that he looked decidedly ungracious. She saw, by his manner, that he suspected that this smooth-spoken Yankee was going to patronize him, though nothing could have been franker and less patronizing than Gaston's whole bearing.

"Thank you," Mr. Somers answered, rather curtly, "I have another engagement."

Louis expressed the hope that he would give

them another day while he was in Washington,
and asked for his address, saying that he would
call upon him.

Mr. Somers, having a hazy impression that
to hand his card was the proper thing, and not
wishing to be outdone in *savoir-faire*, fumbled
in his pocket and produced a tumbled envelope,
out of which he drew a visiting-card of imposing
proportions. Margaret glanced at it quickly,
and saw, to her horror, that it was printed!
In the midst of a wide expanse of tinted paste-
board was inscribed *C. R. Somers*, in aggressive
German type. She smiled to herself, as she
made a swift mental comparison between this
card and another—a pure-white little affair,
with *Mr. Louis Gaston* engraved on it in quiet
script. She knew well what Gaston was thinking of Charley, as he waited quietly while
the latter wrote his address and handed him
the cumbrous card with rather a bad grace,
and she knew as well what Charley, as he
scribbled off the street and number of his
friend's house, was thinking of Mr. Gaston. It

was all very absurd, and she could not help feeling and perhaps looking amused.

Louis lingered to make a few more friendly overtures, but these were so loftily received by Mr. Somers that he soon found it best to take leave, and, with a pleasant "*Au revoir*" to both, he turned and left the room.

"A French-talking, phrase-turning dandy!" said Charley, as soon as his back was turned. "I wonder that you can tolerate such a man, Margaret."

"It would be interesting to ascertain his opinion of you," returned Margaret. "If he puts no higher estimate on your conduct on this occasion than I do, perhaps it is as well for us to remain in ignorance of it."

"And do you suppose I care one penny for his opinion? If you do, you are much mistaken. I was obliged to give my address when he asked for it, but I hope he'll not trouble himself to call. I have no desire to improve his acquaintance."

"And yet you might find it not only pleasant but profitable," said Margaret. "There are many things that you might, with great benefit, learn from him."

"Upon my word, Margaret, this is a little too much," exclaimed Somers. "You have abandoned and repudiated your own people in a very short while, when you can talk of my learning from a conceited Yankee fop like that."

"It isn't the first time I've advised you to take lessons from the Yankees," said Margaret; "and as to Mr. Gaston's being conceited, I really think he's less so than you are, Charley, though he knows much more. As to his being a Yankee—well, yes, he is a Yankee, as we should say, and he's a very capable and accomplished one. And as to the third point, of his being a dandy, you know very well he is simply a remarkably well-dressed man, whose appearance in your heart you admire, in spite of your tall talking. But what's the use of all this? It isn't dress, nor nationality, nor deportment even, that makes the man. Superficially, you two are very unlike, but I think the discrepancy as to your real natures is by no means so great. You are a pair of true and honorable gentlemen at heart—at least, I believe Mr. Gaston to be such, and I know you are, Charley."

She spoke in a tone of great gentleness, for she knew that, before this interview ended, she must say words which would bruise his poor heart cruelly, and it was a kind and honest heart, which had long cherished for her a true and steadfast devotion By degrees she led him on to a quieter mood, and spoke to him gravely and earnestly of their future lives—his and hers—which, as she gently tried to show him, must needs lie apart. He had heard her utter these sad words before, but there was a difference—an absolute resolve in looks and tones that compelled him to realize that this time they were final. And yet she had never been so gentle and so kind.

"I think too highly of you, Charley," she said, when their interview was drawing to a close, " to believe that you will let this feeling for me ruin your life. There is so much a man may do! The very thought of it is tantalizing to a woman sometimes. Oh, Charley, be in earnest. It is all you lack. Do something —no matter what, so it is *work,* and do it faithfully and well. I think that, in itself, would make you almost happy. But don't think about happiness. Indeed, I think that does not signify so very much. Think only of filling your place in the world and doing your duty to God and man, and happiness will come of itself."

When she sent him from her at last, the hope which had until now lived in his bosom was quite, quite dead, never to revive again ; and yet, with the relinquishment of that hope, a new life seemed to spring up within him, which made him resolve, before he left her presence, that he would win her approval though he could never win her love. He knew he could not feel that he had ever possessed her entire approbation, and it was well worth striving for—better, he said to himself, as many another good man has said, in those first moments of sad renunciation, than another woman's love.

That evening Charley Somers formed a sudden resolution. He would not go back to the South and the old stagnating life, which had already made its sad impress upon his mind and character. He would set out at once to South America, to join some resolute fellows who were friends of his, who had gone to seek their fortunes, and had often urged him to come to them. He did not see Margaret again, but wrote her a manly note of farewell, over which she shed tears enough to have recalled him from the ends of the earth, if, by ill-luck, he could have seen them.

It happened that Louis Gaston, chancing to meet her on her way to her room with this letter, which she had just been reading, open in her hand, saw her tearful eyes and pale, distressed face; he further noted traces of weeping that would have escaped a superficial observer, when she appeared at dinner an hour later. He could not help associating these signs with Mr. Somers, and when he took occasion to mention the latter's name, in speaking to Mrs. Gaston after dinner, he was scarcely surprised when she informed him that she had heard, through Margaret, that Mr. Somers had already left for South America, to be gone indefinitely.

"He goes to seek his fortune," said Mrs. Gaston; "therefore I say his return is indefinite."

"And if he finds it," said Louis Gaston to himself, "and the girl he loves consents to share it with him, a man might well envy him. And if she consents not, what will the fortune avail him? It may be that she has already consented! Most likely the sweet pledge has been given, and he goes to seek his fortune with the knowledge that her hopes and fears are entwined about him. What mightn't a man accomplish with such a reward as his in view?"

These reflections passed through his mind, as he sat quietly on one side of the room watching Miss Trevennon as she sat talking to his brother, only her fair, sweet profile turned toward him, and a slightly distressed look on her face, which his searching eyes alone discovered.

CHAPTER XVIII.

A FEW days after Christmas, as Margaret was in her room, writing one of her frequent long letters home, Mr. Decourcy's card was brought to her. It was with a strong feeling of reluctance that she went down to him, and she stopped at Mrs. Gaston's door, hoping her cousin would accompany her. Mrs. Gaston, however, was lying on the lounge, reading a novel, and she declared herself to be too tired to stir; so Margaret was obliged to go down alone.

After her first impulse had died away, she had concluded to keep the locket, as she felt she had no reason to take so extreme a step as to return it. Nothing, however, would induce her to wear Alan Decourcy's picture, and that she meant to let him know.

It was the first time that Margaret had spoken to her cousin since witnessing the scene with Mrs. Vere in the conservatory, and the recollection of that scene necessarily threw a certain amount of constraint into her manner.

Not observing this, however, Mr. Decourcy came toward her, with some words of ardent greeting, and when she extended her hand he made a motion to raise it to his lips. With a movement that was almost rough in its suddenness, Margaret snatched her hand away.

"Margaret! What can this mean?" said Decourcy, in a tone of surprised reproach.

Miss Trevennon gave a little, constrained laugh.

"I don't like that sort of thing," she said, lightly. "Don't do it again. It's unpleasant to me."

"Forgive me," he answered, with the utmost gentleness, untinged by any shade of pique. "I beg your pardon. I am very sorry."

"Oh, never mind! It doesn't matter," said Margaret, hurriedly. "Thank you so much for the locket, Alan. It is lovely—far lovelier than I have any idea of, I dare say, for I am so ignorant about such things."

"I hoped it would please you," he said. "You saw the picture I ventured to put in it? And will you consent to wear it?"

"I don't know about that," she said, somewhat uneasily. "It was very kind of you to put it in, but I never have worn any one's picture. I know you're a cousin, and all that, but I think, if you don't mind, I'll take the picture out and put it——"

But he interrupted her.

"It isn't because I am your cousin, Margaret, that I want you to wear my picture," he said. "On the contrary, I hope for the time when you will forget that relationship in a nearer and tenderer one——"

"Alan! Stop. You must not go on," said Margaret, with sudden vehemence. "There can be no thought of a nearer relationship between us at any time. If we are to be friends at all, this subject must not be mentioned again."

"Forgive me ; I have startled you," he said. "I meant not to do that. I do not want to constrain you or to force this hope of mine upon you too suddenly, but I cannot lightly give it up. It has been with me, during all my wanderings to and fro—if not the definite hope, at least an appreciation of the fact that my sweet cousin was endowed, more than any woman whom I had known, with all the attributes and qualities a man could desire in his companion for life. I cannot, even yet, quite abandon the hope that I may yet induce you to accept my devotion."

Margaret might have borne the rest, but this word galled her.

"Devotion!" she said mockingly, with a little scornful laugh. "Oh, Alan!"

"What do you mean? Why should you speak to me in that tone? It is unfair, Margaret. It is not like you."

"I mean," she said, growing grave, and speaking with a sudden, earnest vehemence, "that you degrade the word devotion, when you call the feeling you have to offer me by that name. I know too well what real devotion means. I have too just an estimate of its goodness and strength to call the cool regard you have for me devotion! A cool regard between cousins does well enough, but that feeling in connection with marriage is another thing, and I had better tell you, here and now, that I would live my life out unloved and alone, sooner than I would wrong myself by accepting such a counterfeit devotion as this that you offer me."

Decourcy, who was, of course, entirely ignorant of the ground on which Margaret's strong feeling was based, heard her with amazement. The only explanation that suggested itself was that some one, who happened to be aware of his rather well-known affair with Mrs. Vere, had informed his cousin. It was, therefore, with a tone of injured gentleness, that he said:

"Margaret, you surprise and grieve me inexpressibly by such words as those. I can only account for them by the possibility of some one's having given you false ideas about me. There are always people to do these things, unfortunately," he went on, with a little sigh of patient resignation; " but you should have hesitated before believing a story to my disadvantage. I would have been more just to you."

" There has been no story told," said Margaret. " If there were any stories to tell, they have been kept from me. Do not let us pursue this topic, Alan, and when we drop it now, let it be forever. It is quite out of the question that we can ever be more to each other than we are now."

" As you have said it," he replied, " my only course is a silent acquiescence. Painful and disappointing as such a decision is to me, since it is your decision I have no word to say against it. But with regard to the lightness and insincerity you have charged me with, I have a right to speak and I must."

Reassured by Margaret's assertion that no one had maligned him to her, he felt strong to defend himself, and it was, therefore, in the most urgent tone that he said :

"I feel it hard, Margaret, very hard, that you should harbor such opinions of me, when my thoughts of you have been all tenderness and trust. Was it not enough that you should deprive me, at one blow, of the hope that I have cherished as my dearest wish for the future, without adding to the bitterness of that disappointment, the still keener one of feeling that I must endure your contempt ? "

There was no doubt of his earnestness now. He was fired by a genuine interest, and he longed to recover the good opinion of this spirited, high-souled girl more than he had longed for anything for years.

"You were never unreasonable, Margaret," he went on, "and therefore I feel sure I may rely upon you to give me your reasons for this change toward me—for you will not deny that you are changed."

"Why talk about it, Alan ? I like you very well. I suppose you're as much to be believed in as other men. The mistake I made was in supposing you to be superior to them. You would not like the idea of being on a pedestal, I know; so be content, and let us say no more about the matter."

"Excuse me, if I cannot consent," he answered, gravely. "It is no light matter to me to lose your regard; and when you remember that I have long hoped to make you my wife, some day, I think you will feel that that fact creates an indebtedness on your part to me, and gives me the right to demand an explanation from you."

His tone of conscious rectitude and the reproachful sadness of the eyes he turned upon her, made Margaret so indignant and angry that she said, with some heat:

"We are playing a farce, Alan, and it had better come to an end. I am perfectly willing to accord you all the credit you deserve. You are a charming man of the world," she added, falling into a lighter tone, "and I admire your manners immensely. I am perfectly willing to continue to be on good terms with you, but there must be certain limitations to our friendship. I could not consent to a return to the old intimacy, and you must not expect it."

"But why?" he said, urgently. "I insist that you tell me. Margaret, remember how important this is to me; remember how I love you!"

And in a certain way his words were true. He felt himself, at this moment, really in love. Now that he found himself likely to lose her, this handsome, spirited, honest-hearted girl, grew inestimably more dear to him. He longed to be able to control her—to settle it, then and there, that she was to be his own. So it was with the fire of real feeling in his eyes that he drew nearer and eagerly sought her averted gaze, and even ventured to take her hand. But the moment she met that look, and felt that touch, Margaret sprang to her feet and half involuntarily took her position behind a large chair, where she stood, resting upon its high back and looking at him with an expression of defiant scorn.

"Margaret," he said, rising too, and bending upon her again that eager look that galled her so, "do you shrink from my mere look and touch? There must be a reason for your manner, and that reason I must and will know."

"You shall!" she answered, excitedly, unable to bear his tone of injured superiority any longer. "I witnessed a scene between you and Mrs. Vere in the conservatory at the ball that night, that made me despise you. It revealed your true nature to me, at a glance, and I am glad of it. I should not have spoken of it. I could have managed to hold my peace and meet you calmly as a casual acquaintance; but that you would not have. But when you presume to offer me what you are pleased to call your devotion, with the memory of that scene in my mind, I can be silent no longer. And now," she went on, after an instant's pause, "I have spoken, and we understand each other.

Let the whole subject be dropped just here, forever."

She had avoided looking at him, as she spoke, and even now she hesitated to meet his eyes. There was a moment's deep stillness, and then, to the relief of both, Cousin Eugenia's silken robes were heard sweeping down the staircase.

She entered, and the room's whole atmosphere changed. Her graceful toilet, well-turned phrases and studious correctness of demeanor, recalled the usages of the world in which they lived, and Margaret and Decourcy resumed their seats and began to talk of snow-storms and sleigh-rides, following Cousin Eugenia's lead.

When Margaret presently glanced at Mr. Decourcy, she saw that he was very pale, but that was all. He had never been more self-possessed.

When he rose to go, Mrs. Gaston, seeing that something was amiss, discreetly walked over to the window for a moment, and Decourcy, taking a step toward Margaret, said in a low tone :

"You have been very hard to me, Margaret, and have judged me hastily. The time may come when you will see that it is so, and for that time I shall wait."

He said good-bye then, without offering his hand, and Margaret, to her amazement, found herself feeling like a culprit. There was such an air of gentle magnanimousness about Mr. Decourcy, that it made her feel quite contrite. In exciting which sensation Mr. Decourcy had obtained exactly the result he had aimed at.

CHAPTER XIX.

IT was two evenings prior to the day fixed for Miss Trevennon's return to her home. January, with its multifarious engagements, had passed, and February was well advanced. It had been a very happy time to Margaret, and, now that her visit was almost at an end, she found herself much prone to reverie, and constantly falling into quiet fits of musing. There was much pleasant food for thought in looking back, but an instinct constantly warned her against looking forward.

On this particular evening, Miss Trevennon and Louis Gaston were alone. Cousin Eugenia had gone to her room, and General Gaston was out. Margaret had observed that she quite often found herself alone with Mr. Gaston lately, and she even fancied sometimes that Cousin Eugenia contrived to have it so. She smiled to think of the multiplicity of Cousin

Eugenia's little manœuvres, and the book she had been reading fell to her lap. She glanced toward Louis, sitting some little distance off at the other side of the fire-place; but he was quite lost to view behind the opened sheet of the *Evening Star*. So Miss Trevennon fixed her eyes on the fire, and fell into a fit of musing.

She was looking her best to-night. There had been guests at dinner, and she was dressed accordingly. Black suited her better than anything else, and the costume of black silk and lace which she wore now was exquisitely becoming. Her rounded, slender arms were bare, and a snowy patch of her lovely neck was visible above the lace of her square corsage. Her long black draperies fell richly away to one side, over the Turkey rug, and as she rested lightly on the angle of her little high heel, with one foot, in its dainty casing of black silk stocking and low-cut slipper, lightly laid across the other, her graceful, easy attitude and elegant toilet made her a striking figure, apart from the distinguished beauty of

her face. Louis Gaston, who had noiselessly
lowered his paper, took in every detail of face,
figure, attitude and costume, with a sense of
keen appreciation, and, as he continued to
look, a sudden smile of merriment curved his
lips. Miss Trevennon, looking up, met this
smile, and smiled in answer to it.

"What is it?" she said. "What were you
thinking of?"

"May I tell you?" he asked, still smiling.

"Yes; please do."

"I was recalling the fact that, when you first
arrived—before I had seen you—I used to
speak of you to Eugenia as 'The Importation.' It is no wonder that I smile now at
the remembrance."

"It was very impertinent, undoubtedly,"
said Margaret; "but I won't refuse to forgive
you, if you, in your turn, will agree to forgive me my impertinences, which have been
many."

"It would be necessary to recall them first,"
he said, "and that I am unable to do."

"I have been dictatorial and critical and aggressive, and I have had no right to be any of these. I have magnified my own people persistently, in talking to you, and depreciated yours. You mustn't take me as a specimen of Southern courtesy. Wait till you see my father. I'm a degenerate daughter."

"I hope I may see him some time. Knowing you has made me wish to know your people better. If I ask you, some day, to let me come and make their acquaintance, what will you say?"

"Come, and welcome," said Margaret, heartily; and then, as a consciousness of the warmth of her tone dawned upon her, she added: "We are a hospitable race, you know, and hold it a sacred duty to entertain strangers. But I fear you would find us disappointing in a great many ways. In so many points, and these very essential ones, we are inferior to you. If only we could both get rid of our prejudices! Just think what a people we might be, if we were kneaded together, each willing to assimilate what is best in the other! But I suppose that is a Utopian dream. As far as my small observation goes, it seems to me that we in the South see things on a broader basis, and that a gentleman's claim to meet another gentleman on equal terms rests upon something higher and stronger than trifling technicalities such as using printed visiting-cards, or calling a dress-coat 'a swallow-tail,' for instance!" she said, with twinkling eyes. "I know you've had those two scores against my compatriots on your mind. Now, haven't you?"

"I will wipe them off instantly, if I have," he said, laughing. "I feel amiably disposed to-night. I think it is the prospect of your departure that has softened me. I hope you are one little bit sorry to leave us. It would be but a small return for the colossal regret we feel at parting from you."

"I am sorry," she said, with her eyes fixed on the fire—"very, very sorry."

"Really?" he said quickly, not daring to

give voice to the delight with which her fervently uttered admission filled him.

"Yes, really. You have all been so good to me. I think General Gaston has even decided to forgive me for being a Southerner, since I could not possibly help it, which is a higher tribute than the regard of Cousin Eugenia and yourself, perhaps, as you had no prejudices to overcome."

"You have paid me the greatest possible compliment," said Louis. "I would rather you should say that than anything, almost. You must admit, however, that at one time you would not have said it."

"That is quite true; but I think now that I did you injustice."

"No, I don't think you did. It was true at one time that I was very prejudiced, and to a certain extent it is true yet; but you've worked wonders with me, Miss Trevennon. I do think I see things more fairly than I did. I had a great deal of hereditary and inherent prejudice to overcome, and I think I have got rid of a good portion of it, thanks to you! Who knows but, if you could have kept me near you, you might have reformed me yet? Of course, I should not venture to criticise a decision of yours, but when Eugenia urged you so, the other day, to stay a month longer, do you know, I almost held my breath to hear what you would say? And your positive refusal quite cut me. It's rather hard on a man, to learn that his education is to be cut short at one fell blow like that; and I am in horrible fear of retrogression."

"Oh, don't laugh at me, Mr. Gaston," said Margaret, rather confusedly. "I am afraid I must often have seemed to you conceited and pert. I believe I am, a little. Even my dear father tells me so, now and then."

"How you love your home and your parents!" said Louis, looking at her very gently. "I have so often observed it. Is it a provincial trait? I never saw a stronger feeling than the one you have for your household gods."

"Yes, I do love them," Margaret said; "and I can give no stronger proof of it than that

Cousin Eugenia's invitation does not tempt me to remain longer away from them."

"And do they love you very much—or not?" he asked, looking into her face and smiling brightly.

"Oh yes," she answered, smiling too; "as if I were perfection."

"I almost think you are," he replied. "I said to myself, from the first, 'She is well-named Margaret, for she's just a pearl.'"

Simply and quietly as he said it, there was something in his tone that thrilled her with a sudden emotion. She dared not raise her eyes to his, and so she turned away her flushed face as she answered, with an effort to speak as usual:

"I am named for my mother. Papa calls me Daisy, to distinguish us."

"I think that suits you almost as well," he said. "Your feelings are so fresh—not a whiff of their perfume brushed away yet. What a thing it would be for one of the careworn, weary worldlings one meets every day, to have

your heart in her bosom for just one hour!
And oh, what a revelation of falseness and hol-
lowness and envy it would be to you to see into
a heart like that! God protect you from it,
Margaret! I am almost glad that you are going back to that quiet old country-place. It
gives me a pang merely to think of the possibility of your being contaminated by the world.
I could not bear to face the thought that the
pearl might lose its pureness and the daisy
wither. I have tried that no one shall suspect
the fact, but you don't know how I have
watched over you. It was presumptuous of
me, perhaps, but now that you know it, do you
forgive me?"

Poor Margaret! She made a brave struggle
for self-mastery, but it was only half successful. Apart from his words, there was something in his looks and tones that made what he
had said a revelation to her. There could be
but one meaning in those fervent, tender eyes,
and the sound of the caressing voice.

"You once refused to shake hands with me,"

Louis went on, presently. "Do you remember? I was in disgrace then, but I can't help hoping I'm restored. Will you give me your hand now, in token of full pardon for the past?"

He had taken a seat very near to her, and when he extended his hand she laid hers in it, without moving from her place. He held it close, for an instant, and then, stooping, laid his lips upon it.

Margaret suffered the caress in silence. She felt nerveless and irresponsible, but her whole nature responded to these signs of tenderness from him. She knew his heart was seeking hers, which was ready to answer, at a touch. She felt confused and tremulous, but very happy and contented and safe, and when she presently withdrew her hand from Louis', she gave him, in its stead, a look of the deepest confidence and kindness.

"There is something I want to tell you, Margaret——" he began, and while she was almost holding her breath to listen, the sound of

General Gaston's key was heard in the lock, and, with a quick motion, they moved apart.

As Louis stood up and turned to meet his brother, Margaret sank back in her seat with a quick sigh. The interruption was almost a relief. The sharp strain of this new-born hope and doubt and wonder was a pain to her, and she was glad to wait. The joy that had been thus held out to her was still to be secured, and she felt a happy safety in the bright future before her.

As for Louis, his pulses thrilled with triumphant hope. All his doubts and misgivings melted like snow beneath the sweet, confiding looks and tones that Margaret had vouchsafed to him this evening. He forgot Charley Somers and all his old mistrust concerning him, and felt happy in the present and almost secure of the future. His ardent blood was stirred as it had never been before. If Mrs. Gaston could have looked into his heart to-night, she could never again have called him cold and unemotional!

CHAPTER XX.

AMES & Gaston had been awarded the
designs for some important buildings, to
be erected at a distance of a few miles from
Washington, and it was in connection with
this matter that Louis Gaston, the morning
after the interview with Miss Trevennon, just
recorded, stepped into a street-car which was
to take him within a short distance of the site
of these buildings.

As he glanced around on entering, he met the
smiling and enticing gaze of Mrs. Vere. There
was a vacant seat beside her, but he did not
choose to take it. His mind, since last night's
episode, had been full of memories and antici-
pations with which the very thought of Mrs.
Vere was discordant. So he merely raised his
hat, in answer to her greeting, and seated himself at some distance from her, near the door,
turning his face to the window. But, as the

car went on toward the suburbs, the passengers gradually departed, and he presently became aware of the fact that only Mrs. Vere and himself remained. Even then his aversion to an interview with her, in his present mood, was so strong that he kept his place, choosing to ignore the fact of their being left alone together. In a very few minutes, however, Mrs. Vere crossed to his side, saying, with an airy little laugh :

"As the mountain won't come to Mahomet——"

Louis, of course, turned at once and resigned himself to the inevitable interview.

"To what fortunate circumstance am I to attribute the honor of Mrs. Vere's society, so far outside the pale of civilization?" he said, adopting the bantering tone he usually made use of in talking to Mrs. Vere, in order to veil his real feeling.

"I am going out to see the Temples," she replied; "I shall have to walk from the terminus. It's such a nuisance having no carriage, and I'm sure I think I deserve one—don't you? But what brings you out so far during business hours?"

"Business," answered Gaston. "I am going to spy out the land for a new building enterprise."

"What sort of building enterprise? I should say a charming cottage, suitable for a pair of domestic neophytes, designed by the architect for his own occupancy, if it were not that a dishevelled young Southerner, with an eccentric tailor and a beautiful voice, stands in the way of that idea! I'm afraid Miss Trevennon, for all her gentleness, must be rather cruel; for, judging by superficial evidences, she has beguiled the wary Mr. Gaston to the point of a futile hankering after Mr. Somers' place. I suppose she has had the conscience to tell you she's engaged."

"Miss Trevennon?" said Louis, meeting her searching gaze without flinching, though his heart gave a great leap and then seemed to stand still. "She has not made me her confidant as to her matrimonial intentions; but if what you say is true, young Somers is a man I well might envy, whether I do or not."

He hated the idea of seeming to discuss Margaret with this woman, and yet he was burning to hear more. He asked no questions, feeling sure that he could become possessed of whatever information Mrs. Vere had, without that concession on his part.

"Oh, there's no doubt about its being true," went on Mrs. Vere. "I happen to know the Welfords, the people Mr. Somers stayed with, very well. Mrs. Welford told me all about it. It seems this young fellow is troubled with a certain degree of impecuniosity, and he had received an offer from some people in South America to come out and join them in some business enterprise, and so he came on at once to consult Miss Trevennon; and it was agreed between them that he should go. The plan is that he is to return a millionnaire and marry her. I wonder she hasn't told you."

"Why should she? Ladies are apt to be

reserved about such matters, however garrulous a man may think proper to be, and Mr. Somers, for one, seems to have been sufficiently communicative."

"Oh, I suppose he only told Mrs. Welford, and she only told me. You must consider it confidential."

"Certainly," replied Louis; "but here is the terminus, and we must abandon our equipage."

He walked with her as far as the Temples' place, which was a very short distance off, and then he bowed and left her with unbroken serenity.

Mrs. Vere was a woman who, in point of fact, was by no means incapable of deep duplicity, but in the present instance she had been guilty only of stating as facts what Mrs. Welford had told her more in the form of conjectures. She had happened to meet Somers at this friend's house one evening, and had introduced the topic of Miss Trevennon, adroitly plying the young man with questions, and had satisfied herself that he was certainly in love with and probably engaged to her. On this basis she and Mrs. Welford had constructed the story which she told with such confidence to Gaston.

As for Louis, he made but little headway with his estimates and prospecting that morning. His first impulse had been to disbelieve this story, and the remembrance of Margaret's looks and tones as he had talked with her last night made it seem almost incredible. But then, as he looked back into the past, he recalled the incident of the pressed flower, and the emotion Margaret had shown on hearing Mr. Somers sing that Christmas night, and the long interview that followed next morning, and, more than all, the traces of tears he had afterward detected; and, as he thought of all these things, his heart grew very heavy.

He soon resolved that he would go at once to Margaret, and learn the truth from her own lips.

When he reached the house, he found Thomas engaged in polishing the brasses of the front door, which stood partly open. Being

19

informed by him that Miss Trevennon was in the drawing-room alone, he stepped softly over the carpeted hall and entered the library. From there he could see Margaret, seated on a low ottoman before the fire, her hands clasped around her knees, and her eyes fixed meditatively upon the glowing coals. How his young blood leaped at the sight of her! How lovely and gentle she looked! Was she not the very joy of his heart, and delight of his eyes? Where was another like her?

He stood a moment silently observing her, and then he cautiously drew nearer, treading with great care, and shielding himself behind a large screen that stood at one side of the fire-place. In this way he was able to come very near without having his approach suspected. He meant to get very close and then to speak her name, and see if he could call up again the sweet, almost tender regard with which she had looked at him last night. Somehow, he felt sure that he should see that look again. He had half forgotten Charley Somers and Mrs.

Vere. He kept his position in silence a moment. It was a joy just to feel himself near her, and to know that by just putting out his hand he might touch her. His eager gaze was fixed upon her fair, sweet profile, and sought the lovely eyes which were still gazing into the fire. He could see their musing, wistful look, and, as he began to wonder what it meant, those gentle eyes became suffused with tears. He saw them rise and fill and overflow the trembling lids, and fall upon a letter in her lap. At sight of that letter his heart contracted, and a sudden pallor overspread his face. He had been so uncontrollably drawn to her that, in another moment, the burning words of love must have been spoken, and the eager arms outstretched to clasp her to his heart. But this letter was in a man's handwriting, and his keen eyes detected the South American stamp on the envelope. His blood seemed to congeal within him, and his face grew hard and cold.

He stepped backward, with an effort to

escape, but his wits seemed to have deserted him; he stumbled against a chair, and, at the sound, Margaret looked up. Oh, *why* were his eyes so blindly turned away from her? *Why* did he not see that ardent, happy look with which she recognized him? Surely it was all and more than memory pictured it! Surely then he must have known, beyond a doubt, that her whole heart bade him welcome!

But he would not look at her. He turned to make his way out, as he had come, pausing merely to ask, with resolutely averted eyes:

"Excuse me, but can you tell me where Eugenia is?"

"In her dressing-room, I think," said Margaret, in a voice that, in spite of her, was husky.

"I want to speak to her," he said, and, without another word or look, he walked away.

Poor Margaret! Her heart was sore and troubled at the sad words of Charley Somers' note. In her own state of happiness and hope, they struck her as a thousand times more touching. She felt restless and uneasy, and she would have given much for some slight sign of protecting care and tenderness from Louis. She was ready to relinquish everything for him. She knew that he could make up to her for the loss of all else; but although he must have seen that she was troubled, he could bear to leave her with that air of cold composure! A dreadful doubt and uncertainty seized upon her, and she went to her room feeling lonely and dispirited.

There was to be a large ball that night, and it was not until Margaret came down to dinner, and observed that Mr. Gaston's place was vacant, that she learned from Cousin Eugenia that he had excused himself from both dinner and the ball. She did not ask for any explanation, and Mrs. Gaston only said that she supposed he had work to finish. No one took any special heed of his absence, but Margaret remembered that it was her last dinner with them, and felt hurt that he should have absented himself; the ball was suddenly bereft of all its delight. She knew there was something wrong, and her heart sank at the thought that there might be no opportunity for explanation between them. But then she remembered the unfinished sentence that General Gaston's entrance had interrupted the night before, and she felt sure that all must come right in the end.

Animated by this strong conviction, and remembering that she would not leave until late in the afternoon of the next day, she dressed for the ball in a beautiful toilet of Cousin Eugenia's contriving, composed of white silk and swan's-down, resolved to throw off these fancied doubts and misgivings as far as possible. In spite of all, however—though Cousin Eugenia went into ecstacies over her appearance, and she had more suitors for her notice than she could have remembered afterward—the evening was long and wearisome to her, and she was glad when Cousin Eugenia came to carry her off rather early, in anticipation of the fatigues of the next day.

When they reached home there was a bright light in the library, and Louis was sitting at the table writing.

"Is that you, Louis?" said Mrs. Gaston, calling to him from the hall: "Margaret must give you an account of the ball, for I am too utterly worn out. Go, Margaret—and lest you should not mention it, I'll preface your account by saying that Miss Trevennon was, by all odds, the beauty and belle of the occasion."

With these words she vanished up the staircase, whither her husband had preceded her.

Half glad and half timid, Margaret advanced toward the centre of the room, and when Louis stood up to receive her, she could not help observing how careworn and grave he looked. There was a troubled expression in his face that touched her very much. Something had happened since last night. She felt more than ever sure of it; and it was something that had stirred him deeply.

"I am glad the last ball was such a successful one," he said, placing a chair for her, and then, going over to the mantel, he stood and faced her.

"It was a beautiful ball," said Margaret; "the rooms were exquisite."

"Were they supplied with mirrors?" he asked, folding his arms as he looked down at her, steadily.

"Mirrors? Oh yes; there were plenty of mirrors."

"And did you make use of them, I wonder, Miss Trevennon? Do you know just how you look, in that beautiful soft gown, with the lovely white fur around your neck and arms? I should fancy it might tempt one to the mermaid fashion of carrying a mirror at the girdle."

He smiled as he spoke—a resolute, odd smile that had little merriment in it.

"What have you been doing, all this time?" she asked, wishing to lead the conversation away from herself.

"Working," he answered; "writing letters —doing sums—drawing plans."

"How you love your work!" she said.

"Yes, I love my work, thank God!" he answered, in a fervid tone. "It has been my best friend all my life, and all my dreams for the future are in it now."

"You love it almost too much, I think. It takes you away from everything else. Do you mean to work in this way always? Have you no other visions of the future?"

"Oh, I have had visions!" he said, thrusting his hands into the pockets of his sack-coat, and bracing himself against the end of the mantel, while he looked at her steadily as he spoke. "I have had visions—plenty of them! They mostly took the form of very simple, quiet dreams of life; for I have already told you, Miss Trevennon, by what a very demon of domesticity I am haunted. The sweetest of all thoughts to me is that of home —a quiet life, with a dear companion—that would be my happiness. Exterior things would be very unimportant."

He seemed to rouse himself, as if from some

sort of lethargy which he dreaded, and, standing upright, he folded his arms across his
breast, and went on :

"But if I had this vision once, I have put it
from me now, and only the old routine remains
—business and reading and a half-hearted interest in society. There is music, but that I
mistrust; it brings the old visions back, and
shows me the loneliness of a life in which they
can have no part. So it is no wonder, is it,
that I call my work my best friend?"

Poor, poor Margaret! Her heart sank
lower and lower, and when he finished with
this calmly uttered question, a little shudder
ran through her.

"I am cold," she said, rising; "I must go."

He went and brought her white wrap from
where she had thrown it on a chair, and with
one of his peculiarly protecting motions he
threw it around her. Then, gathering the soft
folds in his hands on each side, he drew them
close across her breast, and held them so a
moment, as he said:

" Yes, Margaret, you must go. And it is not for the night, nor for the season, nor even for the year ; it is forever. What would you say to me, if you knew we were never to see each other again ? "

"Most likely we never shall," she said, speaking in a cold, vacant way.

" And what will you say to me? What will you give me to remember? "

" I can only say good-bye," she answered in the same dull tone.

" Good-bye, then, Margaret. Good-bye, good-bye, good-bye; and may God Almighty bless you," he said, and she felt the hands that rested against hers trembling. He looked long and searchingly into her face, with a scrutinizing steady gaze, as if he would photograph upon his mind its every line and feature. And then the light folds of her wrap were loosened, his hands fell heavily to his side, and he stepped back from her.

Like a woman walking in her sleep she passed him, her long draperies trailing heavily after her as she crossed the hall and began to ascend the stairs. Her step was heavy and she moved slowly, and Louis, watching her from below with eyes that were wild with longing and lips that were stern with repression, held his breath in passionate expectation that, as she turned at the bend of the stairs, she might give him one last look. But her eyes, as the sweet profile came in view, were looking straight before her, and the tall white-clad figure was almost out of sight when, without willing it, without meaning it, absolutely without knowing it, he arrested her by a hurried, half-articulate call.

"Margaret!" he cried, in a voice that seemed not to be his own, so strange and altered was it.

The weary figure paused, and she turned and looked down at him. A little glimmer of the bright joy, which had been so lately smothered out of life, shot up in her heart as she heard him call her name, but when she looked at him, it died. He was standing with his arms folded tightly together, and a look of the most rigid self-control in his whole aspect. A man that loved her could never look at her like that, she thought, and she felt at that instant, more than ever, that she had deceived herself. Complete weariness seemed to master her. Her chief feeling was that she was tired to death. What was the use of going back?

"I have something to say to you," said Louis, in a voice that was colder than it had been yet. "Come back, for a moment only."

She was very weak, and it seemed easier to comply than to refuse; so, very silently and slowly, Margaret retraced her steps.

As the beautiful white vision drew nearer, step by step, the young man's whole heart and soul went out to meet her, but at the same moment his physical frame retreated, and he withdrew into the room before her, conscious only that he still held possession of himself, and that the spirit within him was still master of the body. Long habit had accustomed him to frequent renunciation. All these years he had been resisting and overcoming, in smaller things, with the conscious knowledge that he was thereby acquiring power which would enable him to conquer when greater temptations should come. And now he knew that his mightiest temptation was hard upon him.

He pressed his arms tighter together across his breast, set his lips and held his breath, as his temptation, clad in a wondrous long white garment, wafting a sweet fragrance and waking a murmuring silken sound, came near to him, and passed him by.

When Margaret had actually moved away from him, and thrown herself weakly into a low, deep chair, and he realized that his arms were still folded, his lips still set, he drew in his breath, with a long respiration that seemed to draw into his heart a mortal pain; and he knew that his practice had stood him in good stead, and that his strength had proved sufficient in his hour of need.

It would have been only for a moment. All he wanted was to take her in his arms an instant, and kiss her just once, and then he could have let her go forever, and counted himself a happy man to have lived that moment's life. That was all; but that he felt himself in honor bound to renounce, because he believed her to be pledged to another man. And he had accomplished the renunciation; but now that this was so, he felt an impatient rebellion against further discipline. The resistless torrent of his love and despair rushed over him, and nothing should keep him from speaking! Words could do her no harm, and there were words that burnt upon his lips, whose utterance alone, it seemed to him, could keep his brain from bursting.

He opened his lips to speak, but the words refused to come. There was a spell in the silence that he felt powerless to break. The room was absolutely free from either sound or motion. Margaret had dropped her weary body sideways in the cushioned chair, with her long white robe sweeping behind her, and her face turned from him, so that only her profile was in view.

The young man stood and looked at her, possessed by the sense of her nearness, enthralled by the spell of her beauty. He could see the rise and fall of her bosom under its covering of silk and fur, and there was a dejectedness in her attitude that made a passionate appeal to his tenderness. She was very pale, and her lowered lids and a little drooping at the corners of her mouth gave her lovely face a most plaintive look. She was tired too; the inertness of the pliant figure, with the motionless bare arms and relaxed, half-open hands, showed that plainly enough. Fragile and slight and weary as she was, how could she endure the battle of life alone, and who, of all men in the world, could strive and struggle for her as he could? The thought of her woman's weakness was a keen delight to him at that moment. He had never felt himself so strong. With a quick motion that emphasized his thought, without interrupting the stillness, he threw out his right arm and clinched his hand with a conscious pleasure in his strength. Nerves and veins and muscles seemed to tingle with sentient animal force.

All these excited thoughts passed through his brain with lightning-like swiftness, but now, at last, the silence was broken by a sound. It was a very gentle one—a short, faint sigh from Margaret; but its effect was powerful. It roused the young man from his absorption and recalled him to reality.

He sat down a little space away from her, and with his fervid eyes fixed on her pale profile and lowered lids, began to speak.

"It was an impulse, not a deliberate purpose, that made me call you back," he said. "I should perhaps have done better to let you go, but I did not, and now you are here, and I am here, and we are alone in the stillness together, Margaret, and you will have to listen to what I have to say. I think you must know what it is. My efforts to keep the truth out of my eyes when I looked at you, and out of my voice when I spoke to you, have seemed to me mis-

20

erable failures many a time, and I dare say you have known it all along."

He paused a moment, still looking at her. There was not a quiver in the still face pressed against the cushions, but at his last words the beautiful arm was uplifted and laid against her cheek, hiding her face from view, as the slim hand closed upon the top of the chair, above her head. It was an attitude full of grace. The white wrap had fallen back, leaving bare the lovely arms and shoulders, and revealing perfectly the symmetry of the rounded figure. Although the face was hidden, he could see every exquisite line and tint of it, in his mind's eye, almost as plainly as he saw, with his actual vision, the soft masses of hair drawn back from the little shell-like ear, and the portion of white cheek and throat which her screening arm did not conceal.

In spite of strong repression, the hot blood overflowed the young man's bounding heart and sent a glow of dark color surging over his face. Something—a little fluttered movement of the breast—revealed to his confused consciousness that Margaret herself was not unmoved. He rose and advanced toward her.

"You know it," he said; "but let me put into words the sweet, despairing truth. I love you, Margaret. Oh, good and beautiful and true and sweet, how could I choose but love you!"

He dropped upon his knees before her, and in this low position he could see her lovely, tremulous lips. At something in their expression a sudden little flame of hope shot up in his heart.

"Margaret," he said, in a deep, commanding tone that was almost stern, while all the time his hands were clinched together, so that he touched not so much as the hem of her dress— "Margaret, look at me. Let me see straight into your eyes."

There was no disobeying that tone, which he now used to her for the first time. She felt herself mastered by it, and, lowering her arm, she showed to him her loving eyes, her trembling lips, her entranced and radiant face.

Instantly his arms were around her, his lips to hers, in an embrace so tender, a kiss so sweet, as can come only in that rare union of freshness and completeness for which all the past lives of these two young souls had been a preparation.

"You were wrong. I did *not* know," she said, presently, breaking the long silence and murmuring the words very softly in his ear.

"Then you have been dull and blind and deaf, my darling, my darling, my darling!" he said, lingering caressingly upon the repetition of the poor little word, which is the best we have to convey the tenderest message of our hearts. "Do you know it now, or do you need to have it proved to you still further? Let me look at you."

But she would not lift her head from its safe and happy resting-place, and her eyes refused to meet his until he said again:

"Margaret," in that stern, sweet voice which thrilled and conquered her; and then she lifted up her eyes, and fixed them with a fervent gaze on his.

"God help me to deserve you, Margaret, my saint," he murmured, as he met that look of lovely exaltation. "It hurts me that you have to stoop so far."

"I do not stoop," she answered. "You have pointed me to heights I never dreamed of. We will try to reach them together."

Later, when their long talk, including the short explanation of their misunderstanding, was over, and they were parting for the night, with the blessed consciousness that they would meet to-morrow in the same sweet companion-ship—with the thought in the mind of each that the future was to be always together, never apart, Louis went with her into the hall, to watch her again as she ascended the stairs.

When she had gone but a few steps, she paused, leaning over the banister:

"Doesn't it seem funny," she said, the serious happiness her face had worn giving place to a merry smile, "such a Yankee and such a Rebel, as you and I! Let us set an example of letting by-gones be by-gones, and shake hands across the bloody chasm!"

THE END.

Stories by American Authors

In accordance with the announcement made at its beginning, this now completed series is a collection of the more noteworthy short stories contributed by American authors in recent years to periodicals, or included in publications for some reason not easily accessible.

The remarkable popularity and critical success which the series has been fortunate enough to gain has more than justified the publishers' belief that American short stories thus brought together would make an extraordinary showing of strong, varied and striking work, the collective interest of which would be for the first time recognized. Now that the collection is finished, it forms one of the most entertaining resources that a lover of good fiction can have at hand.   Taken from a variety of sources, it has drawn from more than one critic the verdict that it is entitled to a more enduring popularity than even its well-known predecessor in the English field, the "Tales from Blackwood;" and the admission that it goes very far to establish the American short story as the most characteristic, original and well conceived of its class.

If the popularity of the isolated volumes is good evidence, the now complete group will have a standard value for the library as the only attempt made adequately to represent this department of our fiction.

This well-chosen series of the best short stories American literature affords.—Boston *Advertiser*.

The collection to be embraced in this series will afford one of the most surprising accumulations of evidence of our literary growth yet submitted to the world, being especially interesting as showing the wealth of good writing recently produced by American writers.—Troy *Times*.

We do not abate our enthusiasm for these stories. They can be relied upon to be the very best.—Hartford *Post*.

They have been selected with excellent judgment, and in bringing this entire collection of sketches together from the various periodicals in which they have appeared the publishers have shown that our literature is more fertile than has been hitherto supposed in writers who have mastered the difficult art of story writing.—Boston *Saturday Evening Gazette*.

The publishers are rendering a public service, and the series is unquestionably destined to become exceedingly popular.—Washington *National Tribune*.

This little volume of short stories by American authors (volume 3) would by itself make the reputation of contemporaneous American literature in any unprejudiced country in the world.—Hartford *Post*.

The publication was begun as a mere experiment. It is now an assured success. The glad welcome given these little lemon-colored volumes may well be a source of honorable pride to the enterprising originators of the series, as it is certainly of gratification to those interested in the permanent preservation of what is best in this department of literature.—Syracuse *Herald*.

This series of Scribners' shows how much good material in the way of old stories may be found in the files of the old magazines. The judgment of the editor has been unfailing in the one main requisite, readableness. We fail to recall a single one of the thirty short stories published which was not interesting, and also worthy of study from an artistic standpoint as a specimen of literary skill.—San Francisco *Chronicle*.

These tales are well selected. They creditably represent many of our most successful and admired tale writers, and afford another and impressive proof of the reluctant admission lately made by the London *Saturday Review*, that the most successful tale writers are Americans.—Hartford *Times*.

The public ought to appreciate the value of this series, which is preserving permanently in American literature short stories that have contributed to its advancement. American writers lead all others in this form of fiction, and their best work appears in these volumes. They ought to be in every private libary.—Boston *Globe*.

Never has an equal number of first-rate short stories appeared in the same compass.—N. Y. *Journal of Commerce*.

The series is a capital one, well edited, and evidently meeting a well-defined desire on the part of the reading public.—Boston *Courier*.

It should have an honorary place in every library, because it is the only undertaking of its kind, and has been carried out with a taste and judgment that have secured the best short stories of American fiction.—Boston *Globe*.

Recent American Fiction

PUBLISHED BY

CHARLES SCRIBNER'S SONS.

GEORGE W. CABLE'S NOVELS.

THE GRANDISSIMES. A Story of Creole Life. With a frontispiece, "The Cabildo of 1883." One vol., 12mo. $1.25.

OLD CREOLE DAYS. With a frontispiece, "The Café des Exilés." One vol., 12mo, uniform with *The Grandissimes*, $1.25.

POPULAR EDITION OF OLD CREOLE DAYS. Two Series, sold separately, 30 cents each. The same in cloth, gilt top, with frontispieces, 75 cents each.

"Here is true art at work. Here is poetry, pathos, tragedy, humor. Here is an entrancing style. Here is a new field, one full of passion and beauty. Here is a local color, with strong drawing. Here, in this little volume, is life, breath, and blood. The author of this book is an artist, and over such a revelation one may be permitted strong words."—*Cincinnati Times.*

MRS. FRANCES HODGSON BURNETT'S NOVELS.

THAT LASS O' LOWRIE'S. One vol., 12mo, cloth, $1.50; paper, 90 cents.

"We know of no more powerful work from a woman's hand in the English language."—*Boston Transcript.*

"The best original novel that has appeared in this country for many years."—*Phil. Press.*

HAWORTH'S. One vol., 12mo, cloth, illustrated, $1.50.

"Haworth's is a product of genius of a very high order."—*N. Y. Evening Post.*

LOUISIANA. One vol., 12mo, illustrated, $1.00.

"Mrs. Burnett's admirers are already numbered by the thousand, and every new work like this one can only add to their number." — *Chicago Tribune.*

GEORGE PARSONS LATHROP'S NOVELS.

NEWPORT. 1 vol., 12mo. Price, $1.25; paper, 50 cents.

"This is undoubtedly the best picture of Newport life that has been given, not only for its characteristic amusements, customs, and individualities, but also its mental, moral, and social atmosphere."—*Boston Globe.*

AN ECHO OF PASSION. 1 vol., 12mo. [New edition.] Cloth, $1.00. Paper, 50 cents.

"The whole story is remarkable for the skill with which very natural and probable incidents are made to present a spiritual conflict."—*The Atlantic Monthly.*

IN THE DISTANCE. 1 vol., 12mo, $1.00; paper, 50 cents.

"'In the Distance' presents unusual ingenuity of plot, and contains sketches of characters which betray an acute observation and an adequate power of expression."—*Century Magazine.*

GUERNDALE. By J. S., of Dale. 1 vol., 12mo. Cloth, $1.25 ; paper, 50 cents.

" After endless novels of culture, here is a novel of power ; after a flood of social analysis and portraiture, here is a story of genuine passion and of very considerable insight of the deeper sort."—*Christian Union.*

" The plot of the story, or rather of the romance, for no other name properly describes it, is full of delicacy and beauty. . . . The author has given us a story such as we have not had in this country since the time of Hawthorne."—*Boston Advertiser.*

THE CRIME OF HENRY VANE. By J. S., of Dale. 1 vol., 12mo. $1.00.

" The author of " The Crime of Henry Vane " has the power of drawing character in a few sharp strokes, and of handling his characters naturally and simply in interesting and logical situations. Moreover, he has the great gift of style. Here is a book thoroughly well thought out and thoroughly well written. Not only are there no slovenly sentences or speeches anywhere in 'The Crime of Henry Vane,' but also there are pungent passages where a just or novel thought is expressed with admirable felicity, concision and point."— *London Saturday Review.*

THE LADY OR THE TIGER? By FRANK R. STOCKTON, author of " Ruddy Grange." 1 vol., 12mo. Cloth, $1. Paper, 50 cents.

" The stories pique the reader's curiosity and entirely absorb his interest almost before he has finished the opening paragraph . . . until he has reached the last page. Scarcely one of the stories do not bear the author's stamp of subtle and delicate fancy."—*Washington National Tribune.*

IN PARTNERSHIP. By BRANDER MATTHEWS and H. C. BUNNER. 1 vol., 12mo. $1.00.

" Many volumes of good short stories have appeared within a year, but none so good as ' In Partnership,' by H. C. Bunner and Brander Matthews. They display a mastery of the theory and technique of story-telling. ' The Documents in the Case,' and ' The Seven Conversations of Dear Jones and Baby Van Rensselaer,' are models of original conception, cunning suggestion, and that brilliant, effective execution, which may convert even a poor subject into a respectable work of art."—*The Nation.*

THE KING'S MEN. A Tale of To-Morrow. By ROBERT GRANT, JOHN BOYLE O'REILLY, J. S., of Dale, JOHN T. WHEELWRIGHT. 1 vol., 12mo, $1.25.

This daring and ingenious story of the future is the most widely discussed book of the season. The brilliant literary partnership which produced it has aroused the keenest curiosity ; and certainly the experiment has been the boldest in the history of literary collaboration. The book is crowded with action and ingenious complication ; and yet the powers which the authors have shown elsewhere are never lost in its rapid movement.

CUPID, M.D. A Story. By AUGUSTUS M. SWIFT. One vol., 12mo, $1.00.

" It is an extremely simple story, with a great and moving dramatic struggle in the heart of it."—*The Independent.*

AN HONORABLE SURRENDER. By MARY ADAMS. One Vol., 12mo, $1.00.

" The story belongs distinctly to the realistic school of modern fiction. The situations are those of every day. The characters are not in the least eccentric ; the dialogue is never extravagant ; the descriptive and analytical passages are neither obtrusive nor too prolix. The sum of all these negations is a charming book, full of a genuine human interest."—*Portland Weekly Advertiser.*

** For Sale by all booksellers, or sent, post-paid, upon receipt of price, by*

CHARLES SCRIBNER'S SONS, Publishers,

743 and 745 Broadway, New York.